Christmas on the Island

Compass Key, book six

Maggie Miller

Second chances do exist.

Five former sorority sisters, all in their 50's, undertake the adventure of a lifetime when a mysterious invite reunites them at an exclusive resort set on a private island.

Olivia was the quiet one. Her divorce from her alcoholic husband freed her in many ways but caused a rift with her daughter that seems impossible to heal.

Amanda was the perfect one. Widowed and desperately broke but hiding it, she needs a new start more than anyone can imagine.

Leigh Ann was the cheerleader. Her ongoing divorce is completely amicable, or so she'd like everyone to believe. The truth isn't quite as rosy.

Grace was the party girl. And she still is, much to the dismay of her husband, who's struggling to keep their restaurant afloat. Grace hopes her time away will give them both the space she thinks they need.

Katie was the brains. Now she's incredibly successful but hiding secrets that could change her life if they were to get out.

When their beloved house mother invites them on an all-expenses-paid vacation, then drops a huge surprise on them, the five friends face a major decision. Can they overcome their pasts in order to take advantage of the amazing future being offered?

Take the journey to Compass Key with them and find out.

Chapter One

 as there anything more stunning than a sunrise in the Keys? Maybe not, although Iris had to concede that the sunsets were rather spectacular, too. And at this time of year, with Christmas only a handful of days away, everything looked even more beautiful.

Pine and holly lighted garland wrapped the railing of the front porch of her three-story home, where she stood surveying what she could see of the island of Compass Key and the sprawling complex of Mother's Resort. Below her was the ramp built to make her home accessible after she'd fallen and fractured her hip.

Now, here she was, some ten months later, not just rehabilitated but better than she'd been before the fall. And looking forward to celebrating another Christmas. Something she wasn't sure would ever happen. All of it was thanks to the care of those around her and some dedicated lifestyle changes. Best of all, she no longer needed a walker *or* a cane.

In fact, she was stronger and more fit, and her mind felt as sharp as it had ever been. She'd even lost thirty pounds! Anyone who didn't believe this place had magic hadn't been here long enough.

Seeing all of the resort before her made it impossible not to smile. There was so much to be happy about and not just for personal reasons. So many wonderful changes had already happened, bringing so much life and vitality to the place.

Now Christmas was right around the corner, and it was going to be the best one she'd had in a very long time. Since her beloved Arthur had passed, that was for sure.

Bringing the girls in had been the smartest decision she'd ever made. Those girls, five of the finest, most wonderful women she'd been a housemother to for the Delta Sigma Sorority, had all accepted her offer to become part-owners of the resort and island.

Her way of making sure her late husband Arthur's legacy lived on by putting the resort and the island in good hands.

What a remarkable job they'd done in these past ten months, too.

Mother's had never had this kind of undercurrent of excitement and energy about it. Even in the peak old days when she and Arthur had been running it, the place had always felt much...sleepier. Laidback and on island time.

Which wasn't a bad thing, Iris thought. Mother's was an exclusive resort on a private island. Those who could afford the resort's hefty price tag came here to relax and escape the often-grueling grind of their lives.

That was still very much an option, but with the new focus on health and wellness, the place had a liveliness it hadn't had before. One of the biggest perks Iris had seen was the increase of younger guests, who she imagined had previously considered Mother's a little too outdated for them.

The younger clientele were just as wealthy—they had to be—but they were also more active than the old-school guests. The resort was now getting more musicians, singers, actors, and social media celebrities. The latter, to Iris, were only famous for being famous. She didn't care, though.

Mother's welcomed everyone.

And according to Katie and Olivia's daughter, Jenny, Mother's had become very popular on social media, thanks to that new, hipper clientele.

In fact, a young woman, a popular singer by the name of Lala Queen, was arriving tomorrow with quite a few members of her entourage to spend two weeks at the resort, where they'd be filming her new music video. With permission, of course.

They'd booked ten of the best bungalows and were,

as Amanda had mentioned, spending a king's ransom on their stay here. Spa and salon packages, special catered meals, personal training, boat rentals—the list went on.

Iris laughed softly. She'd initially had no idea who Lala Queen was, but now that she knew, she imagined the young woman's visit was going to make for an interesting Christmas. But the girls would handle it. They handled everything these days.

Iris couldn't be prouder of them.

"There you are." Vera walked around from the side of the porch where Iris usually sat and had her morning coffee. The housekeeper joined Iris at the railing. "Beautiful day, hmm?"

"Outstanding." Iris stretched her hand out across the vista. "Look at this place, Vera. Look what my girls have done. Buildings repainted and reroofed, carpets cleaned, some brand-new landscaping, better lighting, and that doesn't even touch the new projects—"

"Don't forget Arthur's Marina." Vera tipped her head toward the new ten-slip marina that had been added just to the left of Iris's house.

"No, definitely can't forget that." The marina was for the watercraft of employees only and it had been named after Arthur, because he'd originally wanted to build one there. He'd even had plans drawn up.

Katie had spearheaded that project and what a marvelous job she'd done with it, too. Because of the new slips, the main marina was now free to house more guest boats. Eddie, the boat captain who managed that site with help from Rico, his second-in-command, had also been able to bring in a new glass-bottom boat.

Guests had been raving about the tours he gave on that boat. Iris understood. He'd taken them all out on the boat's maiden voyage and they'd seen a spectacular array of sea life. It was like looking into an aquarium! Iris had regained a sense of wonder about where she lived, something she hadn't even realized she'd lost.

The main marina had gotten some additional kayaks and paddleboards, too. Lastly, the resort had purchased two sea bikes. Iris had been a little skeptical of those. They looked like giant tricycles with enormous balloon tires and were meant to be pedaled on the water like a regular bike on land.

The younger clientele *loved* them. So much, Eddie kept suggesting they buy a third. Maybe they should. But it wasn't up to her. It was up to the girls. And Olivia would have to give her approval that such a purchase would work with the resort's budget, but Iris didn't have much worry there.

The girls hadn't just improved the place, they'd increased prices, just a little, just enough to help cover how much more expensive things were these days.

"You want your breakfast out here, along with your coffee?" Vera asked.

"Yes, I think that would be lovely. Then I've got that tour of one of the new family bungalows at ten. I'm meeting the girls over there and they're going to take me through." The family bungalows were another new addition to the resort. Built on some of the island's untouched acreage, the family bungalows were two- and three-bedroom accommodations with their own pool complex that included a lazy river.

There were two new dining spots being added as well. A second full-service restaurant, as yet unnamed, and something Grace and her husband referred to as a "fast-casual" eatery, to be called Castaways. The whole area was currently being called Phase II, but would eventually be known as Mother's East.

"Oh, I'd love to see how they're coming. Mind if I tag along?"

"Please do. I think Katie and her sister are coming, too." They lived on the floor above Iris, while Nick, Arthur's son, lived on the top floor with his girlfriend, Jenny. It was so nice having the whole place full. Iris loved the feel of being in the midst of everything.

"Are the new bungalows still on schedule?"

"I think they're close," Iris said. "Amanda's supposed to update us on all of that today. The pool area still needs a lot of work, I know that."

"It's going to be really something when that all opens in another month or two. New bungalows, new pool, new restaurants."

Iris nodded. "It's so exciting, isn't it? I know the girls are itching to take reservations for them, but Olivia and Amanda both agreed they should wait until things are further along. Just in case there's a snag."

"I never imagined this place could get better," Vera said. "And yet, here we are on the brink of a brand new chapter." She shook her head and sighed. "Arthur would be amazed."

"And proud, I think." Iris stared at the marina that bore his name, Arthur's handsome, smiling face on her mind.

"Definitely proud," Vera said. "Now, let me go grab your coffee and get to work on your breakfast."

"Thank you." Iris left the railing to take a seat on the rattan sofa. Her three cats, Calico Jack, Anne Bonny, and Mary Read, named for the pirate who'd once made this island his home and the women he kept company with, were all nearby. They'd already had their breakfast.

Such spoiled creatures. Iris smiled. *And such darling companions.*

Calico Jack jumped up to sit on the cushion beside her.

"Hello, my darling boy. Don't you look handsome this morning." She scratched under his chin, making him purr. "Aren't we lucky to live here?"

"We are," Vera said as she came back out with a cup

of coffee. She put it on the table in front of Iris. "Bacon and eggs all right this morning?"

"Perfect," Iris said.

Kendall, the holistic nutritionist Leigh Ann had hired in August, had, with Dr. Nick's approval, written up an anti-inflammatory eating plan for Iris.

She sipped her coffee, sweetened with stevia and lightened with a splash of heavy cream. Now her meals focused on good protein, higher fats, low-glycemic vegetables, and occasionally fruit. It had taken some getting used to, but Iris felt like a new woman. She especially attributed the strength of her body and the clarity of her mind to the new way of eating.

She also did yoga three times a week and walked regularly. She loved walking on the boardwalk that Owen Monk, the billionaire who lived on the other end of the island, had built.

He'd done it to make it easier to get to Katie, his girlfriend. Well, fiancée. He'd proposed to her at Thanksgiving. That boardwalk made it easier for her to get to him, too. But they all enjoyed walking on it. Just like the marina, the boardwalk was for employees only. It wouldn't do for Owen, who was something of a celebrity himself, to be inundated with curious guests.

But what a lovely walk it was. It went right past the ruins of the pirate Calico Jack's old fortress. Twice a week, there was a guided nature walk that took guests there to have a look for themselves. But that's as far as they went.

Vera returned with Iris's breakfast. "Here you are. Two eggs scrambled with goat cheese, two strips of bacon, and a couple slices of avocado."

"It looks wonderful, Vera."

"Thank you. More coffee?"

"No, I'm good." Iris was more than good. She was fantastic. Just like life on Compass Key.

Chapter Two

Grace sipped a cup of coffee as she sat on the front porch of her bungalow and looked at the menu samples, trying to decide which one she liked the best. David would have to weigh in, too, but he was still sleeping. He'd be up soon, though.

Today was jam-packed with work to do for both of them and the list seemed to grow every day, but he had several great candidates for the chef he'd be hiring to run the new fine-dining restaurant. Jonas, one of the line cooks at The Palms, would be taking over as the chef at Castaways, the new fast-casual eatery that would allow guests to grab a quick bite or even pick up food to go.

It was all coming together.

The front door opened, and David leaned out, rumpled from sleep. "Morning."

"Hi, honey. How'd you sleep?"

He chuckled softly. "I dreamed I ran a shrimp

special for dinner, but there was nothing but calamari in the kitchen." He scrubbed a hand over his face. "I told the line cooks no one would notice."

Grace laughed. "Some of the guests might not." She got up from her seat and pointed to his. "Sit. I'll get you some coffee."

He took her hand as she came toward him and gave her a kiss. "You're awfully sweet this morning."

"I have an ulterior motive." She gestured to the folder she'd left on the small table between the two chairs. "I want you to make a decision about the new menu design."

He smiled. "Maybe that should wait until after I've had my coffee."

"Coming up." She slipped past him and went to the kitchen, poured him a mug of black coffee, and rejoined him on the porch.

He had his feet up on the railing, and the menus splayed out on his lap. "These all look pretty good, but I'm leaning toward this one."

He tapped his finger on the one with a simple line of gold foil across the top and the restaurant's name in an elegant script.

She put his mug on the table and smiled. "That's the one I liked, too."

He put it on top of the other two, tucked them back into their folder, and set them down so he could drink his coffee. "Are you telling Iris today?"

Grace nodded. "We are. And she'll see the sign as part of the big reveal, which should be fun."

"That was a great idea you had. And it's a heck of a Christmas gift."

"Speaking of, what do you want for Christmas?"

He shook his head, holding his coffee mug toward the view. "What else could I want? Look at our life. We live in paradise. I'm the head chef of a fantastic restaurant, overseeing the opening of a second one. And let's not forget about the cookbook."

Grace grinned. "How could I forget any of that? You dedicated it to me, which was about the sweetest thing ever." With the help of Katie's agent, David had landed a fantastic cookbook deal. He and Chantelle, the pastry chef, had worked like mad to create the recipes for it. The publisher had sent a photographer to Compass Key to take pictures of the food and the book had been rushed into production so it would be available for the Christmas season.

The Island Life Cookbook had been released only a week ago and was, as agent Maxine had punned, already making waves.

"That reminds me," David said. "Chantelle and I need to sign a few more copies of the book for the gift shop. Do you know they're selling an average of fifty copies a week in there? Apparently, it's become the number one gift people take home for their friends."

"Doesn't surprise me at all. Especially not with Christmas coming up."

"Back to the gift thing." He took another sip of his coffee. "How about you? What would you like?"

She opened her mouth, trying to think of something. "I don't really know. My needs are pretty much met." She smiled. "Just having a day off together will be the gift."

"I'd agree with that."

She looked at the time. "I should get my shower. I have interviews starting at ten."

"Front of the house?"

"Yep. For both locations."

"What would you like for breakfast, sweetheart?"

Having a chef for a husband had its perks. "I would love a veggie omelet."

"How about a veggie omelet with a little chorizo in it?"

"Sounds great. Light on the onions and garlic, though. I don't want to breathe that all over the people I'm interviewing."

He smiled. "Got it. You go shower, I'll get in the kitchen."

"You don't have to, you know. I can grab a bowl of granola."

He shook his head. "You deserve better. And you're going to need your protein with the day you have ahead of you."

"Thanks, honey." She took her cup in, set it by the coffeemaker, then went upstairs to get showered and ready for the day.

After she got out and was doing her makeup, she heard him puttering in the kitchen. He had music playing. He'd found a station on his streaming service that played island music. It had quickly become his thing. She liked it, too. It really was the perfect soundtrack for their life.

She pulled on tan pants and her new Mother's Resort staff shirt. The change from polo shirts to the lighter-weight tropical button-downs had been Amanda's idea. Grace was all for it. The Hawaiian-styled shirts with their white background covered in turquoise and pink flowers and green leaves were bright and cheery and more flattering than the polos. The soft rayon was definitely cooler than the knit fabric, too.

Although cooler wasn't really a concern this time of year, when the weather seemed to hover around a constant seventy-six degrees during the day. All the same, she added a lightweight turquoise cardigan, because she'd be in the air conditioning most of the day.

She finished her look with pebbled-leather white slip-on sneakers, a pair of gold hoops, and her watch.

Happy with her reflection in the mirror, she

grabbed her purse, tucked her phone into it, and headed downstairs.

David had just put a plate on the counter for her. "Your breakfast is served."

"Looks fantastic." She took a seat and admired the gorgeous omelet he'd made for her. He'd garnished it with a little salad of halved cherry tomatoes and feta cheese with olive oil and fresh herbs. She picked up her fork.

He set a manilla folder and a travel mug of coffee on the counter. "For you to take with you. Those are the resumes I liked the best, but obviously you'll be interviewing them in person, so that will really help with the decision-making then."

"I'm curious to meet them." David would do a final interview with anyone she'd okay'd for the kitchen or a management position. She dug into her food. "I feel very spoiled."

He smiled proudly. "Good."

She ate quickly, in part because she needed to get going but also because the food was so good, then ran back upstairs, brushed her teeth, and finally headed for the door, purse over her shoulder, notebook and files in one hand, her travel mug of coffee in the other.

David walked with her, giving her a kiss goodbye. "See you later?"

She nodded. "I'll stop by after the interviews are

over and let you know how they went. I'm really
hoping to find some good people today."

"I hope so, too. If we're really going to open The
Palms to off-island guests, we're going to need the help.
For all three places."

"I know." Allowing a few select reservations at The
Palms for non-guests was something they hoped to put
into practice at the start of the New Year.

"Well, you always excelled at the front-of-the-house
stuff. And were a good judge of character. I know you'll
find a great crew."

"Fingers crossed." She left the bungalow and
walked through the staff common area, cutting across
toward the other side of the island where Phase II was.
She couldn't wait until it was actually open. It was
going to be so beautiful.

An employee pathway had been laid in pretty early
to allow access. It was gated at the end near the guest
bungalows with a clever design that looked like
bamboo but was actually weather-proof aluminum.

The gate wasn't locked or secured with any kind of
code. Just a sign that said Staff Only. If a guest really
wanted to come through, there was nothing to stop
them, but people didn't come to this island to misbe-
have. They came to be pampered and treated like
royalty.

Which was fair, Grace thought, considering what
they were paying.

The new family bungalows would be no different. The three-bedroom rented for twelve grand a night, the two-bedroom for ten. Expensive, yes, but actually a better deal per person than the original bungalows.

Of course, those all looked out directly onto the beach.

These bungalows were being billed as water view, which they were. Built up on taller stilts much like Iris's house, there was no shortage of blue visible from their windows, but they weren't directly on the beach. Their views also included the new pool complex and a lot of greenery in the back, much like the original bungalows.

Just like those, these also had their own private hot tubs, but bigger, designed to hold four to six people.

Interviews were being held in the new fine-dining restaurant, which was still being completed, but at this point it was all small stuff. Tables and chairs had already been brought in. In another week, David would be spending some time in this kitchen, getting it up and running so that it was completely operational in about a month's time.

She set up near the back of the restaurant where a wall of windows looked out onto a lush tropical garden and an artificial waterfall that would help create some of the flow for the lazy river when it was finally turned on. It was a gorgeous setting and the perfect backdrop.

Workers drifted in and out. There was still some

touch-up painting to be done, a few light fixtures that needed to be installed, that sort of thing.

She checked the time. Her first interview should be arriving. She sat down to wait, looking over her list of appointments.

"Grace?"

She looked up into a familiar face, but not one she'd seen in years. Or been expecting. "Curt?"

He nodded, smiling. "That's me."

She looked at her appointments again. The first one was listed as Macarthur. She paged through the list of resumes David had given her. Sure enough—it wasn't a mistake. The top one in the folder bore the name Curtis Macarthur.

She stared at the man before her, all kinds of thoughts, questions, and emotions going through her. "Curt Macarthur."

His brows lifted. "I wasn't sure you'd remember me. How are you?"

"I-I'm great." How could she forget him? "What are you doing here?"

He held his hands out. "What else? I'm applying for a job."

Chapter Three

"That's it," Leigh Ann said softly, directing the woman on the yoga mat. "Just sink down into the pose, letting your mind and body work as one. Really feel how you can open up into the stretch and try to relax into it. Give in and don't fight it."

The guest on the mat in front of her was actress Rita Harlow, a fixture of the long-running daytime soap opera, *Beyond Tomorrow*. The show had recently moved to a streaming channel, where it hoped to find a new audience.

Rita had come to Compass Key for ten days of wellness and rejuvenation before the start of the new season began and she'd had a private yoga session with Leigh Ann every morning and a weight training session every evening in an attempt to put the finishing touches on her personal revitalization, as Rita had been calling it.

Leigh Ann knew that before arriving at Compass Key, Rita had gotten some work done. An eye lift, a full-face laser resurfacing, and some fillers. Possibly more than that, but most of the bruising and redness was gone.

Leigh Ann felt for Rita. It was clear she was a talented actress, but also one who very much felt the pressures of her industry and the high value placed on youth and beauty.

"Very good," Leigh Ann said. "Now lie back in *savasana* and breathe out any tension you might still be holding. Let the ground support you."

Rita shifted position to recline on the mat, arms out at her sides, palms up. For a woman in her mid-sixties, she looked remarkably good, extra work aside. She was in fantastic shape, which Leigh Ann expected would only improve during her stay at the resort.

Rita was also following the anti-inflammatory diet that Kendall, the new holistic nutritionist, had recommended. It was the same one she'd put Iris on and clearly the diet had worked wonders for her. Rita seemed to be enjoying it. In three days, she'd dropped two pounds and declared her energy had never been better.

Leigh Ann was thinking about trying it herself. "Breathe deeply and allow your senses to join in peaceful harmony. Become one with the air around you, the ground beneath you, and be supported by that unity."

Leigh Ann quietly walked to the narrow table by the studio's entrance, waited a few moments, then gently tapped the cloth-wrapped mallet against the meditation gong, sending a deep, calming peal through the room to announce the session was over.

"Open your eyes when you feel ready."

Rita took a deep breath and slowly sat up. "That was wonderful. As always."

Leigh Ann nodded. "Thank you. You're progressing very well. I know this isn't your first time doing yoga, but you should be pleased with your progress."

Rita got to her feet. "I am. Absolutely. I wish I'd booked for a full two weeks now. In fact, I might stop by the front desk and see if I can't extend my stay. This is exactly what I needed before heading back to that rat race." She smiled quickly. "Which I love. But that schedule can be taxing."

"I'm sure it is." Leigh Ann offered her a bottle of water from the small fridge kept just for that purpose. "Enjoy the rest of your day. I'll see you at four."

Rita took the bottle. "Thank you. See you at four."

Leigh Ann cleaned the yoga mat, rolled it, and put it away, then turned off the music and the lights, locked up and did a walkthrough of the fitness area to make sure it was in good order as well.

She smiled at the handful of guests working out.

Towels needed straightening, so she took care of that, along with putting away a few of the free weights that hadn't been returned to the rack after being used. The fifty-pounders were an effort.

One that reminded her she'd considered hiring a full-time fitness center attendant to handle these sorts of things, but it had seemed like something she could easily take care of. And it was. But if she continued to take on more private sessions with guests, it might not be. Plus, it would be helpful to have a male trainer on staff to meet all of the guests' requests.

Not all of the men wanted to work out with a woman, and she understood that.

She walked back to her bungalow, in need of something more substantial than the cup of coffee and container of yogurt she'd started her day with. She had about thirty minutes before she needed to meet everyone at the new Phase II restaurant for the big reveal.

Her mouth curved in a smile just thinking about it. She unlocked her door and went in, going straight to the kitchen. She flipped on the lights, although the bungalow had a nice amount of natural light already.

She pulled eggs, butter, and some smoked salmon cream cheese from the fridge. She added butter to a pan on the stove, then cracked three eggs into a bowl and whisked until they were nicely mixed. She used her salt and pepper grinders for a little additional seasoning, then put the eggs into the pan along with a spoonful of the cream cheese and gave the eggs another stir. The cream cheese would melt into the eggs, making them extra delicious. The quick scramble would hold her until lunch, which probably wouldn't be until one.

She was meeting Grant at his studio, and he was bringing lunch. No idea what he might have made, but she was sure it would be good. He was a great cook and always picked wonderful and interesting ingredients. The thought of seeing him kept the smile on her face. She was crazy about him. Even better, he was crazy about her and made no attempt to hide it.

Her fingers went to the large silver pearl dangling around her throat. His gift to her on her birthday. A reminder, he'd told her, that she was his sea goddess.

There was no way she'd forget that, however. His new series of paintings, a sort of crossover between the dream world, the underwater world, and reality, all featured her as the model.

In the first painting, one he was soon to finish, she was a mermaid dreaming of wings that appeared to be sprouting from her back, except they were clouds. She sat on a rock, surrounded by the sea while flying fish sailed past.

In the next painting, she'd be walking in the sand beside a beautiful tranquil sea while the night sky above her was filled with constellations all in the shapes of fish and sea life.

She shook her head to bring herself out of her thoughts. The eggs were nearly done. She gave them a good stir with her silicone spatula.

While they finished cooking, she got a mineral water out of the fridge and leaned against the counter to check her schedule. She was giving a stretch class at two, but that was it until Rita's next session at four.

Which was good. Leigh Ann still needed to spend a little time at Aqualina, the spa, to have a look at how things were going there. She liked to make an appearance at least once a day, doing her best to touch base with Manuela, the managing esthetician, about any concerns she might have.

Since putting Manuela in that new role officially, the number of appointments for facials had doubled, mostly because Manuela had started a program that used a series of three facials to rejuvenate and refresh the skin. It was proving to be very popular.

The new product line Manuela had recommended was selling well, too, but Leigh Ann wasn't sure if they were displaying it as much as they should be. Was it too pushy to feature it in the spa's reception area? All of the guests came in through there, meaning they'd at least get to see it once that way.

Of course, the spa was already an add-on experience, outside of the one complimentary massage all guests were offered. Most guests who visited the spa spent an average of five hundred dollars. Perhaps if the product lines were better displayed, that check might be increased a little.

The resort's goal was to give guests the best experience possible, but providing that experience didn't come cheaply. And Leigh Ann wanted to be sure the spa and fitness center were doing their part to contribute.

The salon certainly did. Since bringing in some new nail technicians, new stylists, and making sure the existing ones were up-to-date on their education, the salon was holding its own and then some.

She gave the eggs one last stir, then turned them out onto a plate, which she put on the counter. She put the pan and spatula in the sink to handwash when she was done eating. She took her seat and tucked into her breakfast.

When she was finished, she put her fork, dish, and mixing bowl in the dishwasher, then handwashed the pan and spatula she'd used, setting them out on a drying mat.

She ran upstairs, checked her hair, makeup, and brushed her teeth. Being around Rita had gotten Leigh Ann thinking more about her own appearance.

She did her best to keep herself in shape. Not that hard to do when she was so active, but with every passing year it became more of a battle. She watched what she ate, not really limiting herself too much, but generally trying to keep her portions to a reasonable size.

Maybe she should give Kendall's eating plan a try.

Leigh Ann leaned closer to the mirror, smoothing the skin between her brows, then touching the soft lines around her eyes.

There was probably more she could be doing. Well, for certain there was. But should she? Grant never did anything but compliment the way she looked, but she was her own harshest critic. What woman wasn't?

Manuela had mentioned several times that the top requests guests had was for injectables such as Botox and facial fillers, along with laser treatments for hair removal and skin resurfacing.

Some of the exact kinds of things that Rita'd had done. The kinds of things that so many of their guests did on a regular basis.

Should the spa offer them?

And if they did, could Nick do it? He was a doctor, after all. Of course, he'd spent the bulk of his professional years taking care of people in countries that needed medical care the most. She wasn't so sure he'd suddenly want to shift his attentions to the lifestyles of the rich and famous.

She sighed. She supposed it couldn't hurt to ask, but it already felt like something he wouldn't want to bother with. It was so superficial. And yet, for a woman like Rita, it seemed like the thing that gave her the kind of confidence she needed to do her job.

Maybe for Rita it was even a little bit of a necessity.

Sad, Leigh Ann thought, that the world put so little value on the natural process of a woman's aging. How unfair that men got to age gracefully, embracing their silver hair and character lines while women were surrounded by products and devices meant to keep age at bay for as long as possible.

She put her hands on her hips and stared at herself, pursing her lips. She looked fine. No, she looked better than fine.

Maybe that's what the spa and fitness center should focus on. Glorifying the process of aging well. By taking care of oneself, obviously.

Although, was that being too precious about it? If people wanted to spend thousands of dollars to battle the natural aging process, why shouldn't Mother's get a piece of that?

She shook her head. This was probably going to be her decision. She was the manager of the spa and fitness center. If she wanted to increase the services they offered, that was going to be up to her.

The rest of the women would agree with what she thought was best.

She just didn't know what that was.

Chapter Four

Amanda sat at the desk in the office behind the front desk and looked over the bookings for the week of Christmas. They were completely sold out, which wasn't that unusual. According to what Iris had told them, Christmas had always been a very popular time on the island. Especially for their guests who lived in colder climates.

She could understand. She was loving the climate this time of year. Low humidity, perfect temperatures, lots of sun. It was gorgeous. Being booked seemed a given.

Granted, nearly half the resort was going to be taken up with Lala Queen and her accompanying guests.

Amanda had some doubts about that group. They seemed exactly the type who'd come here believing the money they'd paid meant they could do anything they liked. Which was not the case.

Regardless of how much they were spending, their stay would not be allowed to impinge on the enjoyment and relaxation of the other guests at the resort.

What kind of a name was "Lala Queen" anyway?

Carissa, the front desk manager, came in from her spot at reception. "Did you see? Mr. and Mrs. Carlisle will be spending Christmas with us." She smiled. "It's their fiftieth wedding anniversary. Their children booked the trip for them and are planning to surprise them with it during a big party. I just talked to their daughter who wanted to see if we could do a little cake for them their first night here."

"A little cake?" Grinning, Amanda shook her head. "We can do better than that."

"That's what I told her, but I wanted to talk to you first before I made any promises."

"Let's make sure there's a bottle of champagne in their room, along with our special fruit and chocolate basket. What bungalow are they in?"

"Seven."

"Make a note that the bungalow should be decorated with fresh flowers. Including rose petals on the bed."

"All right."

"And I'll speak to Chantelle myself about doing a cake for them. Maybe I can do it on my way back from Phase II. Do we know what they like?"

"Their daughter said they both love fruit. And lemon cake."

"I can work with that. Fifty! Imagine!"

"I know," Carissa said.

Amanda flattened her hands on the desk. "Can we do a banner, too? Didn't we do a banner for someone a couple months ago?"

"Jorge and Anette Lunden. That Norwegian couple."

"Excellent recall. Let's go with a banner for the Carlisles, too."

"You got it." Carissa leaned in and tapped her fingernail on the monitor to indicate another reservation. "And then there's this."

Amanda glanced at it. "Michael Gideon and Kit Tellman. First-time guests to Mother's." He was an older action star with the rugged good looks to match, and she was a retired supermodel-turned-actress who was slowly making a name for herself as a real force to be reckoned with. She had the kind of big eyes that made her almost seem supernaturally beautiful. Their wedding had been plastered all over social media this summer. Amanda shrugged. "We've had celebrities here before. What am I missing?"

Carissa hesitated, reluctance written all over her face. "I do not approve of gossip. But I've heard some things. Mainly that their trip here is a last-ditch effort to save their marriage. I worry that if things don't go well for them, we could be looking for additional accommodations for one of them."

Amanda straightened. "That bad, huh?"

Carissa nodded. "Kit's assistant made the reservation and I'm pretty sure she didn't mean to share as much as she did, but I can't stop thinking about it."

Amanda looked at the names on the computer screen. "What if we start them off with the honeymoon package? Champagne and chocolate-covered strawberries. And let's see if we can set them up with a couple's massage at the spa. But check in with Kit's assistant again and see if there's anything else they might like."

"I will." Carissa grinned. "I love that you're a romantic. Although considering who you're dating, I can't say that I blame you."

Amanda smiled. She never really had been a romantic. Until Duke. Being with him had made up for so much. Being around his family had helped, too. They were wonderful people. Kind and affectionate. Something her own mother had never really been known for. "Well, I also believe in doing what's in the best interests of our guests and if we can tip the scales in their favor, why not?"

She stood and grabbed her purse, fitting the long strap across her body. "I'd better get going. Text me if you need anything."

"Will do."

Amanda slipped out of the main building and

started walking toward the new development. What a beautiful day.

The path took her past the marina. She waved to Eddie and Rico, who were both at work cleaning the boats. It was time the resort hired another marina worker, she thought. Maybe just a part-time one. But when Phase II opened, there would definitely be an upswing in water activities. Especially if they got more families with children. They might need a boat captain for the glass-bottom boat all by itself.

One of the things that Amanda had suggested was that the original pool be designated as adults-only. They'd all agreed on it, too.

A lot of people who came to Mother's wanted the kind of peace and quiet that didn't include kids screaming, "Marco Polo," or splashing water on them when they were trying to enjoy their pool time.

She doubted any of the children who stayed here would be interested in visiting the original pool anyway, not when the new pool complex was going to have two slides, a lazy river, and a large shallow area with three canopied play spots for shade.

The three outbuildings beyond the marina were just ahead. Grant's studio was one of them. But she took the new path just in front of the first one. That path was not yet open to the public and a yellow rope with a sign reading Staff Only was hooked across the way. She unhooked it, went through, and put it back in place.

The landscaping had already been done. She walked down the path lined with foxtail palms, ginger, crotons, and birds of paradise. There were fruit trees mixed in, too, and torches had been put in place as well, although they were not yet being lit in the nightly ritual. That would only happen when the area was open to guests.

The Phase II bungalows and resort buildings came into view, along with the pool complex. It was so good to see it, even though she'd just been over here a few days ago to check on the progress.

A handsome man in a tool belt approached her, the smile on his face and the gleam in his eyes making her happy she'd come over a little early. "Have you come to check my work?"

She stopped in front of him. "Does it need checking?"

Duke leaned in and kissed her. "I don't know. You tell me."

She put a hand on his chest for just a moment. As much as she loved the hard muscle underneath his T-shirt, it wouldn't do for the other workers to see them being unprofessional. "I think your work is just fine."

"Fine? I guess I'd better try harder." He winked at her, making her smile.

"How's it going?"

"Great. I'll probably jinx us by saying this, but we're slightly ahead of schedule in a few areas."

"That is great."

He nodded. "Bungalows A, B, and C will be ready for occupancy by next week."

"Really?"

"Yep. Doesn't mean they can be, though. We still need our inspection certificates, but other than that, they're done. With the holidays, inspections probably won't happen until after the first of the year."

"That's all right." She looked past him. "I see the sign is up on the restaurant." It was covered with a tarp.

He glanced over his shoulder. "That happened first thing this morning. We had to make sure it was done for Iris's visit."

"Which should be any moment."

Grace stepped out of the restaurant and gave Amanda a wave. Amanda waved back.

"Go on," Duke said. "Get back to work. I need to get up there for the big reveal."

"Okay. Have a good day."

"You, too, babe."

She almost let out a small laugh of pure giddiness. No one had *ever* called her babe. It filled her with a kind of lightness she'd never known before. Floating a little, she headed for Grace.

"Wait up," a voice called.

Amanda stopped and turned. Olivia was headed toward her. "Hey."

"Hi there. How's it going?"

"Good," Olivia said. "Busy."

"Same here, but I'm excited to see all of this. We're getting close."

"We are," Olivia said. Her brow furrowed as she looked ahead. "Does Grace look a bit upset to you?"

"She does." Amanda instantly wondered if something was wrong in the building or if Grace was having an issue. She asked as soon as they reached their friend. "You okay? You look bothered. What's wrong?"

Grace shook her head, looking a little off. "Nothing exactly. It's just been a weird day." She sighed and put her hands on her hips. "Curtis Macarthur showed up as my first interview today. It really threw me. It's my own fault. I should have looked closer at my list of interviewees."

"Curtis?" Amanda felt like she knew that name for some reason.

Olivia sucked in a breath. "*The* Curt?"

Suddenly, Amanda opened her mouth as the recollection came to her. "Isn't he the guy you were engaged to in college before David?"

Grace nodded, her expression strained. "Yes. The guy who broke my heart into about a million pieces when he just disappeared without a word."

"What on Earth was he doing here?"

"He saw David's cookbook, did some digging, and found out we were here. He's been in Florida a while, apparently, and managing a large barbeque place in Key Largo."

"So the interview was legit?"

Grace nodded. "Yes."

Olivia made a face. "But you're not going to hire him. Are you?"

Grace sighed. "I don't know. He's really well-qualified. It might also be opening a can of worms."

Amanda nodded. "I'd say. One that expired a long time ago."

Chapter Five

Katie was vibrating with nerves. Nerves that had nothing to do with the big surprise they were about to unveil to Iris.

In approximately seven hours, the son she'd given up for adoption, his wife, and their two children – her grandchildren – would be here for a week. Owen was flying them in and putting them up in one of his guest houses. Which she could get to in about six minutes on her bike, thanks to the new boardwalk that linked Owen's end of the island with the resort end.

She glanced at the enormous square diamond on her hand. Knowing that Owen loved her so much he'd asked her to marry him was a very calming feeling.

She exhaled. It wasn't like she hadn't met her son and his family before. She'd taken a couple of days off in July and gone to visit them in Texas. But having them here was going to be a little different. They'd be meeting Owen for the first time. And her sister, Sophie.

It was all so exciting.

"You ready?" Sophie called out.

"On my way." Katie put her sunglasses on and went out to meet her sister in the living room. "Inside steps or outside steps?"

"Inside," Sophie answered as she put her coffee mug by the machine to use again later.

Fabio, their cat, was perched in his cat condo watching a bird in one of the nearby palm trees. He certainly seemed to have adjusted to island life easily. But then, so had Sophie. Katie had worried about her sister being too much of a city girl to be able to settle down here, but her relationship with Gage, Owen's security guy, had gone a long way toward giving Sophie some new interests.

The two were spending more and more time together. They'd even started working out together, which sounded like torture to Katie. Gage was former military, and his exercise routine was no joke. But Sophie was clearly up for it, and judging by the dress size she'd lost, it was working.

Katie and Owen preferred movie nights. Although now that she could ride her bike between their houses, she had to be getting more exercise than in the old days when she did nothing but sit in front of her keyboard, pounding out her next bestseller.

Which reminded her that for at least a few hours today, she needed to get some words written.

Katie turned toward the stairs that would take them down to Iris's floor, which was right below them. A door and partial wall had been installed not just there but at the stairs that led up to the third floor as well. In part for privacy, but also for noise. With all three levels occupied, they'd quickly realized it was necessary.

As they descended, Katie called out, "Iris, we're on our way down."

She appeared at the bottom of the steps, looking beautiful in a red and green caftan. "Hello, my darlings. I can't wait to see the new bungalows."

Katie nodded, smiling. If only Iris knew how much more there was to see. "Me either."

Vera joined them and they all went out Iris's front door. They took the path toward the resort, past Arthur's Marina, then cut in toward the staff quarters, which gave them an opportunity to look at the four new bungalows going up there.

"When will those be ready again?" Sophie asked.

"Sometime in the next few weeks, I think," Katie answered. "As you know, the goal is to make them available to some of the new hires, especially since Castaways is going to be open for more hours than any other place in the resort."

Two of the new staff bungalows were laid out

differently than the traditional ones so that they had four bedrooms and four bathrooms. Those two were meant to be shared by four employees in a roommate situation, enabling the resort to have more onsite staff.

From the staff quarters, they followed the path through to Phase II. Grace, Amanda, Leigh Ann, and Olivia were all gathered up ahead, looking very much like they were deep in conversation.

Katie called out to them. "Hey, guys."

Olivia gave them a wave. "Hi there."

As the two groups melded and everyone said hello, Katie leaned in toward Leigh Ann. "You all looked like you were having a pretty serious conversation just a second ago."

Leigh Ann nodded. "We were. Grace was just telling us her ex-fiancé showed up for a job interview this morning. David set it up, as his resume was one David had pulled as a potential candidate for the manager position."

Katie looked at Grace. "David didn't know who he was?"

Grace shook her head. "I've only ever called him Curt, and to be honest, it's been a long time since I've talked about him. A long time. Like years."

"Wow," Sophie said. "That had to be weird."

Iris snorted. "I'll say."

"It's all right," Grace replied. "I got through the interview just fine."

"Good." Olivia clapped her hands to get everyone's attention. "All right, I know we're here to have a look at the new family bungalow, but first, there is something else we need to take a peek at." She turned toward Iris. "Mostly, that *you* need to take a good look at."

Iris touched the enormous diamond at her throat. A gift from her late husband, the Escape Diamond rarely left her person. "Me?"

"Yes, you," Olivia said. "Follow me."

She led them past some of the giant Queen palms that had been installed some time ago, and around to the front of the new fine-dining restaurant.

Duke stood on the roof. He waved at all of them. "Morning, ladies."

Iris grinned. "I've seen Duke before, but it's not a bad way to start the day."

They all laughed.

Katie snorted. "Pretty sure that's not what Olivia meant, Iris."

"It wasn't," Olivia agreed. "But this is." She waved at Duke. "Go ahead."

He bent down to do something and, a moment later, the tarp fell away from the sign, revealing the name of the new restaurant: Iris's.

Iris pressed her hands to her cheeks. "Oh, you girls. I can't believe you did that." She sniffed. "You girls are too much."

Even Vera looked weepy.

Leigh Ann put her arm around Iris. "Merry Christmas, Iris."

Iris let out a sob. "First Arthur's Marina, now this." She hugged Leigh Ann, kissing her cheek. She made her way around to all of them, doing the same. "I love you all so much. Thank you. I wish Arthur could see what a fantastic job you're all doing."

Grace shrugged. "Maybe he can."

Olivia was all smiles. "I'm so pleased you're pleased."

"Same here." Katie laughed. "And not just because if you hadn't liked us naming the restaurant after you, replacing that sign would have been pretty expensive."

More laughter and chatter ensued until Amanda got their attention. "What do you say we go have a look at one of our new guest accommodations? I think you're going to be pleased all over again."

"Lead the way," Katie said. She was ready to get moving. Not that she didn't want to see the bungalow —she did—but the sooner she could get back, the sooner she could get to work on the book that was due in a month.

After finishing up her last series, she'd decided to start with a brand-new idea. One that used Compass Key as the inspiration.

That idea was romances set on a small, tropical island resort. *Real* romances that focused on the emotional journey of the hero and heroine more than just the sexy times. She didn't really care if her readers liked the books less because of it. Being with Owen had changed her. Shown her what love was. Just like living on Compass Key had changed her. She wanted to reflect those new ways of viewing life in her stories.

But in order to create some distance between her real home and the island she was now writing about, she'd set the island in the South Pacific and named it Kalema. But much like Mother's, the resort specialized in catering to the rich and famous, although there'd be plenty of not-so-rich-and-famous women to be the heroines, too.

Katie knew her readers loved a good rags-to-riches, damsel-in-distress story, especially when that damsel was swept off her feet by a dashing billionaire.

"Earth to Katie. Come in, Katie."

Katie blinked at her sister. "What?"

"You looked like you were somewhere else entirely."

Katie laughed. "I was. Kalema."

Sophie grinned. "Thinking about the new series, huh?"

Katie nodded. "I can't help it. You know how I get when I'm excited about a book."

"I do, and I think it's a great sign. But try to focus for the next couple of minutes or you're not going to remember anything of what's around you, and this is not a place you want to forget. Just *look*."

Katie realized they'd walked into the small foyer of the family bungalow. Could this really be it? The place was stunning. She'd seen the concept drawings but seeing it in person was something else entirely.

The floors were tiled with big, creamy squares of polished limestone, but the wall that faced the foyer was what stopped Katie in her tracks. Tiled with tiny deep blue and teal glass tiles, the wall gleamed as if the sea had been captured in each little square.

A narrow dark wood table sat before it, a large, stand-mounted nautilus shell the only decoration. But with a wall like that, you didn't need much.

To one side of that wall were steps. She followed Sophie through to the other side, where the bungalow opened up into the living area with a smaller dining and kitchenette space and then the two bedrooms and two bathrooms. The same limestone floors continued on, with the furnishings in deep blue, teal, and vibrant green to match the entrance wall and all the plant life visible through the windows.

Touches of bright coral and vivid yellow added some unexpected color. Lush fabrics such as silk and chenille made everything so inviting, while grasscloth covered the walls, adding a real sense of the tropics and plenty of texture.

"This is amazing," Katie said. "Who came up with this?"

Amanda and Leigh Ann both raised their hands. Amanda nudged Olivia. "Come on, you helped."

With the shrug of one shoulder, Olivia stuck her hand up, too. "I only helped a little."

Leigh Ann rolled her eyes. "She helped a lot."

"I'm so impressed," Katie said.

"So am I," Vera said. "This is gorgeous. No one who stays here is going to want to leave."

Iris clapped her hands. "You girls have outdone yourselves. The old bungalows look so shabby now."

Leigh Ann laughed. "They do not. But these places have to be impressive. People are spending serious cash to stay here. Their experience needs to be a little mind-blowing. Which reminds me, you all really need to see the master bedroom upstairs. Or at least what we're calling the master."

As if on command, they all turned, went back to the foyer, and trooped up the steps.

Katie knew immediately why Leigh Ann had wanted them to see this. The cream limestone was still present here, but it continued up the wall behind the bed all the way to the ceiling.

And what a ceiling it was. The whole thing had been painted the deep blue of a tropical night sky and then the constellations had been picked out in metallic gold.

She put her hands on her hips to stare up at it.

"Okay, that is going in a book. That is a wow factor if ever there was one."

The rest of the room was completed in more shades of dark cobalt blue and cream with dark wood furniture and accents in gold and mother of pearl. From the sliding glass doors that led out to a small balcony, the view of the water was spectacular.

Katie looked around some more and smiled. The lamps that hung on either side of the bed from the ceiling looked like jellyfish.

She was so blown away she almost forgot she had her phone with her. She whipped it out and started taking pictures. "I love those lamps. I love all of it. The ceiling, the lamps, the view from the balcony, the whole vibe. This is stunning."

Leigh Ann, Amanda, and Olivia were grinning. Leigh Ann pursed her lips. "You should see the bathroom.

They all crowded in, although there was actually room for all of them in there. The back wall of the glass shower mimicked the foyer wall, completely covered in tiny glass tiles, this time in deep blue with the addition of gold-gilded tiles in the pattern of a wave.

"That's it," Katie said. "I'm moving in."

Iris nodded. "I might come with you."

Chapter Six

Olivia was overjoyed by the reception the family bungalow was getting. She knew the design scheme was much more dramatic than the original bungalows, but she believed that would help balance out the fact that these accommodations weren't beachfront.

Granted, these bungalows did have a spectacular private lounging area in the back, which the girls hadn't even seen yet. Or the downstairs bedrooms, for that matter.

She broke into the ongoing conversation about how wonderful everything looked. "Let's go downstairs and check out the other bedrooms, bathrooms, and the backyard space."

That got them moving.

While they all explored the two bedrooms and bathrooms, which were decorated as pairs in either vibrant green or teal blue, Olivia went over and pulled the sheers back from the big slider that made up the rear wall of the bungalow.

The sheers would help keep some of the heat out during the hottest months, but the glass had also been treated to block a lot of UV rays, not just to keep the heat down but to help prevent the bungalow's interior from fading.

Something she'd never thought too much about when she'd lived in Ohio.

As the women filtered out of the bedrooms and bathrooms, she went ahead and opened the big sliding door. The three-paneled glass slider went all the way back and pivoted on the curved track. That allowed the doors to slide out and against the bungalow's exterior wall, meaning the entire rear wall was open. This made the back deck feel like an extension of the living room.

In the cooler months like now, being able to walk right outside into all of that open space and fresh air was something special.

Olivia held her hand out toward the deck. "Here it is. The outdoor living space."

The deck held a glass-topped dining table with six chairs on one side and a seating area with a glass chunk firepit on the other. From there, wide steps led to a brick-paved patio where the hot tub and more seating options waited, including chaises for sunning along with an umbrella.

And because this was billed as a family bungalow, there was a hammock stand complete with a brightly colored woven hammock. All of it was surrounded by expertly done landscaping that provided privacy from the bungalow next door and shots of color from the birds of paradise, ginger, plumeria, crotons, hibiscus, and heliconia.

"You could just live out here, couldn't you?" Iris said as she took it all in, hands clasped before her.

"I could," Grace said. She closed her eyes and inhaled. "I can smell the plumeria and that little bit of salt in the air that reminds you just how close the water is."

"I give this whole place a ten out of ten," Sophie said. "Will all the family bungalows look like this?"

Olivia nodded. "The two-bedroom units just have a slightly smaller footprint, with only one bedroom and bath downstairs, but yes, just like this model. Same furnishings in the same colors."

A knock on the front door made them all look toward the front of the bungalow. "I'll get it," Vera said.

She went to see who it was and returned with Jenny, Olivia's daughter. She waved at them all. "This *place*. Am I right? My mom showed it to me the other day. It's so good. I mean, it's perfect. And I cannot wait until we can get this up on social media. There are some travelgramers that are going to lose their minds over this."

Olivia smiled. She'd showed Jenny the bungalow early because she'd wanted a young person's opinion. And Jenny wasn't one to hold back. "We're pretty close to being ready to go public with Phase II." She looked around at the rest of them. "Jenny has promised to help us promote it and get the word out online."

Iris raised her hand. "What are travelgramers?"

Jenny answered. "People on Instagram who basically make a living sharing their travel adventures through beautiful photos and videos. Their goal is to make everyone else want to be where they are."

Iris nodded thoughtfully. "Should we get one of them to come here?"

Jenny grinned. "I think Lala Queen's presence is going to take care of that for you. In fact, I think you should show her this bungalow and see if you can't get her to shoot part of her video here."

Olivia's brows went up. She hadn't thought about that. "You think so?"

"Sure," Jenny said. "What better way to show off this new island palace than in a music video that's going to get millions of views? That ceiling upstairs needs to be seen. People will be dying to know where her video was shot." She glanced around at them with a sly grin. "And I'll make sure to tell them."

"How?" Leigh Ann asked.

"By sharing the word on the resort's social media platforms, but also by haunting the comments section of Lala's social media. When someone asks where it was shot, I'll be happy to tell them."

"They won't be able to afford it," Amanda said. "Not many of them, anyway."

"No," Jenny agreed. "They won't. But a lot of her peers will. And trust me, celebrities watch music videos, too. Word will spread about how next-level this place is."

Olivia nodded. "I hope that's true. We really need to be solidly booked for Phase II to pay for itself. This was not a cheap venture."

"I can imagine," Jenny said.

It was also a little scary to think that for the first time in the history of Mother's, they were going to allow children. If that backfired, they were in trouble. Olivia didn't like taking big financial risks, but she also knew without risk, there was no reward.

And Mother's needed to expand and modernize if they were going to keep new and old clientele on the books. It was the only way.

"Listen," Olivia said. "While I have you all here, there's something I'd like you to start thinking about."

"What's that?" Katie asked.

"The future," Olivia answered. "At some point down the road, the old bungalows will need to be refurbished. That's just an inevitability."

"How soon?" Grace asked.

"That really depends on how well Phase II does. If

it doesn't book out, it'll be a while before we do anything else. If it's a hit, we might be looking at as soon as the year after next to begin redecorating."

Grace nodded. "Good to know. I'd like to add that David and I both think The Palms could benefit from a little makeover, too. Nothing too over the top but it needs freshening up. Once Iris's and Castaways are open, we could probably manage all right if The Palms shut down for a week or two. Just throwing that out there."

"I'll make a note of it," Olivia said. "Anyone else want to add anything to this impromptu business meeting?"

No one said anything, so Olivia spoke again. "All right, then. Let's go have a look at a few more areas in Phase II." She hesitated. "That is, if you want to see more."

"We do," Iris said. "Come on, girls. Let's go."

Grace shook her head. "I'm sorry, I have another interview in fifteen minutes. You all enjoy the rest of your tour. See you soon."

They said goodbye to Grace, and then, with a smile, Olivia led them out of the bungalow and to the games area near the beach section of the pool. "There will be a row of cabanas here that back up to the palm forest area and, in front of them, the games area with giant-sized checkers, connect four, and a playground area consisting of swings, climbing area, and a slide."

"When will all that be in?" Leigh Ann asked.

"End of next month. If not sooner," Olivia answered.

"And when will the pool be complete?" Iris asked.

"Within the next few weeks," Olivia said. "Although again, that could go in either direction by a week or two. Building a project of this size is not an exact science." She turned to point back toward the pool complex. "As you can see, the walkways over the lazy river are just about complete. Those will become gentle waterfall grottos for the rafters to pass through."

"Now that," Iris said, "is something I might have to try out."

They all looked at her. Vera's brows were raised. "You're going to go on the lazy river?"

"Why not?" Iris said. "I can be lazy. All you have to do is sit in a tube and float." She looked at Olivia. "Right?"

Olivia nodded. "That's about the size of it."

"See?" Iris said. "I can do that." She wiggled her finger at Olivia. "Sign me up to be a tester."

Olivia laughed, so happy that Iris wanted to get involved. "I'll put you on the list."

Chapter Seven

As Iris walked back to her house, she felt blessed in a way she couldn't quite describe.

She'd honestly believed the girls had been struggling to name the restaurant. She'd never imagined they were going to name it after her. What an incredibly kind and caring thing to do. The gesture had touched her deeply.

There was more to what she was feeling, though. She pondered it, thinking through what she was experiencing. She realized it was a sense of pride in her girls but also a feeling of special privilege. Like she was getting a glimpse into what their future would be, long after she was gone.

It both humbled and pleased her. The resort would be here, flourishing, well after she was reunited with Arthur.

"You're awfully quiet," Vera said.

"Sorry. Just thinking."

"Care to share?"

Iris took a breath. "I'm a little overwhelmed, to tell the truth. In a good way. They've done so much. Put so much thought and planning into what they're doing. I'm so happy to hear how they're thinking ahead. It gives me great peace."

"I'm sure it does." Vera smiled. "They're intelligent, capable women. You shouldn't be surprised by all that they've accomplished."

"I'm not. Not really. Just so very much in awe of them."

"You were exactly like them, once upon a time."

Iris smiled. "Those were the days, hmm? Although sometimes I don't believe I was ever that young."

"Neither do I," Vera said.

Iris chuckled. "I must say, I feel a lot younger lately than I have in quite a while. These changes have done me wonders."

"Both of us," Vera said. "I never slept so soundly as I have since we started the anti-inflammatory plan."

Iris glanced over as they approached the house. "Speaking of, what's for lunch?"

Vera laughed. "A scoop each of tuna salad and organic whole milk cottage cheese on mixed greens with steamed cold green beans, niçoise olives, and hardboiled eggs with a light vinaigrette."

"You've really taken to this new plan, haven't you? Sounds lovely. Maybe afterwards I can find someone to run me into town." Iris shook her head. She didn't want to be a bother, but she needed to get to the mainland. "I haven't finished all of my Christmas shopping."

"You should get the girls to hire a third boat captain. There's no way Eddie and Rico will be able to keep up when Phase II opens."

"No, you're right. Maybe even two more. Or one full- and one part-time. I'll send them all an email about it after lunch."

They went up the steps together. Iris almost never took the ramp unless it had been a long day. Then sometimes her joints were still a little achy. Even exercise and clean living couldn't completely overcome the aging process. Unfortunately.

Vera unlocked the door. "Do you have a lot of gifts left to buy?"

"Not too much. Just a few things."

A voice called down to her. "Iris?"

She took a few steps out onto the ramp and looked up to the third-floor balcony. She waved. "Hello, Nick. How are you?"

"All right." But he didn't sound all right. And the way he shook his head said he was anything but. "Do you have a minute? I need to talk to you."

"Of course. Come down."

"On my way." He disappeared from view.

She and Vera went inside. The cats were all either under or near the Christmas tree in the corner of the living room. Only Calico Jack could be bothered to give a little meow in greeting. Iris took a quick look. At least there were no ornaments on the floor so far today. The cats seemed to think the tree was there for amusement purposes. Naughty beasts.

"Lazybones," Vera muttered at the cat with a smile on her face. "Maybe Nick will want to stay for lunch. I won't prepare anything until I ask him."

"That would be nice if he could join us. We could eat outside. Shame to waste this lovely weather."

He knocked on the door a couple of seconds later.

"Come in," Iris called.

He came through. "Afternoon, ladies. I hope I'm not disturbing anything."

"We just got back from touring the Phase II project and were about to have lunch," Iris said. "Would you like to join us?"

"I'd love to, but I just got a call from Eddie. He's bringing a guest in with a jellyfish sting." Nick looked at his watch. "I only have about twenty minutes before they arrive. How was the tour?"

It was such a blessing to have him here, Iris thought. "The tour was fantastic. You really should go over and see what the new bungalows look like." She grinned suddenly. "They named the new restaurant after me."

He smiled and nodded. "Hey, that's great. What a nice thing to do."

"I agree. It really was." But she was wasting his time. "What did you want to talk to me about?"

He took a deep breath. "Today has been quite a day. My mother called this morning. She's insisting that she see me for Christmas. She more or less insinuated that I'm being brainwashed by all of you and if she doesn't see me, that proves it and she's going to create trouble. Which you know she's capable of."

Vera snorted and rolled her eyes, then busied herself with taking things out of the refrigerator.

"Indeed. Another threat of a lawsuit?" Iris pursed her lips. They'd been down this road once already. Iris's lawyer had put an end to it all pretty quickly with the promise of a countersuit. He'd been Arthur's counsel originally and Iris believed he was a much sharper attorney than any Yolanda Oscott could afford.

Nick raked a hand through his hair. "Anything's a possibility with her. But I know her and if she says she'll make a stink, she really will do it." He huffed out a breath. "She'll probably start a Mother's Resort Is Brainwashing My Son Facebook group."

Iris cringed inwardly. The last thing the girls needed was bad press. Even from a woman with a reputation as a known gold-digger and pot-stirrer. It wouldn't do to have even a whiff of trouble. Not with them trying to make Phase II a smash hit.

Iris thought and thought hard. It *was* Christmas. And after the morning she'd had, she was feeling rather generous. "Fine. Tell her to come. She'll have to stay with you, though. The resort is booked. And she'll have to behave."

He looked surprised. "Are you sure? I mean, thank you, but don't give in to her on my account."

"Nick, you may not have the best relationship with her, but she is your mother. And maybe if she sees how well you're doing here, and how honestly lovely all of my girls are, and gets to meet Jenny, who is equally lovely, maybe then she'll finally understand how happy you are. It might be exactly what she needs to see."

"Let's hope so. I haven't told Jenny about this yet. That's going to be a whole other bridge to cross. Thanks again, Iris. You're the best. I promise my mother will behave. I'm going to make sure she knows she's my guest and not a guest of the resort. I don't want her thinking she can take advantage of her stay here."

"Thank you." Iris would have no compunction about telling Yolanda the same thing, if need be. She would not let a woman like that push her around.

He headed for the door. "I really appreciate this."

"I know you do. Just like I appreciate your presence here at the resort." He'd saved her life when she'd fallen. If he needed his mother to visit, this was at least something Iris could do to repay him.

"I'll call her on my way to the office. I'll let you

know what her travel details are as soon as I find out, so there won't be any surprises. Not while she's here, either."

"I'm sure it'll be fine." Iris wasn't sure of that. But letting Yolanda visit seemed like the best possible solution.

Iris just hoped it didn't end in the worst possible outcome.

Chapter Eight

Grace did have another interview, but she also needed a few minutes to talk to David. He should be just about walking into The Palms kitchen. She went back into Iris's restaurant and stood in the far corner, away from the workmen, to make her call.

He answered right away. "Hey there. How's it going?"

"It's going all right. I need to talk to you about one of the resumes you gave me."

"Yeah? Which one?"

"Curtis Macarthur."

"Oh, right. I really liked that guy. Solid resume with a serious amount of experience managing restaurants. I don't know why he'd want to leave his current work, but maybe the lure of island life is too strong. Anyway, we'd have to call his references, obviously, but he was pretty much a sure thing for me. I thought we might be able to use him to oversee the management of both Castaways and Iris's. What did you think of him?"

She took a breath. "He looks great on paper, but the thing is..." She wanted to pick her words carefully so that it didn't sound like she cared more than she did. Not about Curt, anyway. Of course, she *did* care. But more in the way that it might create problems between her and David.

And after the rough spot they'd just been through, all because of her drinking, she didn't want to be the reason they went through another rough spot.

"Grace? You still there?"

"Yes. Sorry. Just thinking. Hey, is there any way you could come over here? This is a conversation better had in person, I think."

He chuckled softly. "Sure, but now you've got me thinking I should be worried. Should I be? What's going on?"

"There's nothing for you to be worried about. I'll explain everything when you get here. I have an interview in about ten minutes, though, so you might have to wait until that's over."

"On my way."

She hung up and saw a young woman walking toward her.

"Hi," she said. "Sorry, I'm early."

"No, that's fine." Grace smiled. "Please tell me your name and have a seat. We'll get things underway."

David showed up twenty minutes later, right after the interview. Grace was still making a few notes about the young woman.

She closed the folder and got up to greet her husband. "Thanks for coming over."

"It's really coming along, isn't it?" He looked around, smiling. "I can't wait to get into that kitchen." He rubbed his hands together. "So, what did you want to talk to me about?"

She gestured to the table as she took her seat. He sat across from her. "Curtis Macarthur and I have history."

David's brows went up. "You've worked with him before?"

She understood the supposition. The restaurant industry tended to be something of a small world. It wasn't uncommon for people to know each other from previous employment or through chefs they'd worked for. "No. Curtis, or as I've always called him, Curt, is my ex-fiancé."

David sat back, his gaze suddenly distant, like he was searching his memory banks. His brows lifted again. "*He's* the guy you dated before me? The one you never wanted to talk about?"

She nodded.

"Sweetheart, I had no idea. I never would have pulled his resume if I'd known. Of course, we are talking about something that happened thirty-some years ago. Are you still bothered by all of that?" David grinned. "You do have me now, you know."

She smiled. "Yes, I do. And I don't know if I'm bothered, exactly, but it was a shock to my system to see him. He just disappeared on me back then. Not a word. Things were pretty much perfect one day, then the next he was gone."

"Did you ask him what happened?"

She shook her head. "No. I was so surprised to see him that I just ignored the obvious question and went straight into the interview."

"But he knew who you were."

"Oh, for sure. How many other Graces could he have been engaged to?"

"Good point. So what do you want to do?"

She sighed. "He's one of the most qualified people who's applied. I would have pulled his resume if I were you. I mean, I would have pulled his resume myself if he'd been anyone else. The thing is, we're trying to do what's best for the resort. Is it shortsighted of me to judge him now by the past? And what if..."

She looked through the wall of glass to the waterfall. It was going to be so pretty when it was operational.

"What if he still has feelings for you?"

"That was a silly thing for me to think. Like you said, it's been thirty-some years. I'm sure he barely thinks about me. And if he'd really had feelings, the time to act on them would have been 1989." She smiled at David. "Do you think we should hire him?"

"Will you be uncomfortable around him?"

"It might be a little weird. At least at first."

David tapped his fingers absently on the table. "I don't want you put in a weird situation. I don't want *us* put in a weird situation. I'd love to bring the guy on, but not at your expense. Maybe I should talk to him."

"Now see, *that* would be weird. What are you going to do? Ask him why he didn't marry me? Ask him what his current intentions are?" She snorted. "I'll talk to him."

"Whatever you decide is fine with me." He leaned in. "I mean that. This guy might be exceptionally qualified, but this place is our home. We need to protect it."

He took her hand. "You matter more to me than anything else."

"Thank you." She smiled, a little more in love with him than she had been just a second ago. "I'll let you know how it goes."

He stood up, pulling her with him. "I'm glad he didn't marry you." He brought her hand to his mouth and kissed it. "My life would have turned out very differently if he had."

"I love you. I'm glad he didn't marry me, too."

He kissed her on the mouth, then let go of her. "I'd better get back. Let me know how things go."

"I will." She watched him leave. She had other

interviews today. Four more. But now she also needed to call Curt.

That was going to be an awkward call, no question about it. He'd think she was calling with news about the job. Instead, she'd be asking him to explain himself. Did it matter what he said? Could she work with a man who had betrayed her so deeply all those years ago?

She wasn't sure she could ever really trust him. But that felt like such a petty response, caused by her own lingering hurt. She'd be lying if she said his abrupt disappearance didn't still hurt. It did. She'd had no closure.

Maybe talking to him would give her that closure and let her move on for good.

For all she knew, he was a happily married man and really didn't think about her.

She checked the time. One more interview to go before she had an hour break for lunch and whatever. She'd call him then.

Thirty minutes later, Grace pulled out Curt's resume and dialed the number listed. She was a little nervous about the call, but he was the one who had some explaining to do.

"Hello?"

"Curt?"

A pause. "Grace."

He'd recognized her voice. "Yes. Listen, I need to talk to you a bit more—"

"A second interview? I didn't expect to hear back so soon. As it happens, I'm still at the resort. I can come back over."

"You're still here?"

He laughed. "Confession time. I was just sitting on the beach, thinking about what my life would be like if I actually got this job."

That wasn't the confession she needed from him. "I'm still at the restaurant if you'd like to come back."

"I'm on my way."

He showed up ten minutes later, still dressed as he had been for the interview in trousers, dress shirt and tie, although the tie was considerably looser than it had been the first time she'd seen him.

He was all smiles. She wasn't and, to his credit, he picked up on that. "I'm not here for a second interview, am I?"

"You're here because I need some answers about why you disappeared on me all those years ago. Not long, I might add, after you gave me an engagement ring."

His gaze dropped to the ground and his body language changed, the confidence he'd walked in with gone. "Do you mind if I ask what you did with the ring?"

"A year later, I sold it and used the money to pay for my books."

He nodded. "I'm glad it went to good use." He looked up, making eye contact for a brief moment before looking away again. "I screwed up, Grace."

"That's an accurate assessment. Why?"

His gaze finally came back to her. "I was scared. It hit me all of a sudden that I was about to be a husband and I wasn't even sure about my major. How was I going to support a wife? It seemed like...a death sentence. Please don't take that personally. My head was in a bad place. I didn't even want to be in school anymore."

"Apparently. Where did you go?"

"I went home to Arlington. My parents were pretty mad, as you might expect. They gave me an ultimatum. Go back to school or get a job or move out."

"And?"

"I got a job at a little diner in town washing dishes. Two years later I was the assistant manager. Five years later, I bought the place. I'd found my thing in life. I was happy."

She'd seen it on his resume. The Drive-In Diner. "So that's all it was? You couldn't handle the impending responsibilities of marriage and you ditched? Why not talk to me?"

"I knew you'd be mad. I knew I had no real excuses." He shook his head. "Grace, I could barely look at myself in the mirror. Trying to explain myself to you would have been like asking me to scale Everest. I didn't have the skillset or the strength. I am so sorry about what I did to you. I'm glad things have turned out so well for you. I truly am."

She nodded. "I am, too. Why did you really show up here today?"

"For the interview. I swear it." He smiled. "I also knew it would be a chance to see you and talk to you and maybe make amends. Earlier, though, you didn't seem like you were interested in talking to me about anything but the job, so I just let it go. I'm glad you called me back. I understand if you have hard feelings toward me. I deserve them. I just wanted you to know what happened had nothing to do with you."

Since they were being honest, she wasn't done talking. "I blamed myself for a long time, you know. I thought I'd done something to make you leave."

"I'm sorry. That had to be a terrible thing to deal with. If I could change things, I would."

"I wouldn't. I fell for David because he knew the right things to say to make me believe in myself again. And I don't really have any hard feelings toward you. I did at one point." She laughed. "I hated you."

He put his hands up. "I earned that."

She felt nothing for him. Maybe a little sorry for him that he'd screwed up his life so badly, but then he'd come out of it all right, too. "Why do you want this job?"

"I sold the diner about ten years ago. I got a great offer I couldn't turn down. I always told myself that I'd retire someplace warm. I ended up working for a place that was in danger of going under, turning it around and making it profitable again. I've done that time after time after time now and while it's rewarding work, it's hard. Long hours, too. I'm not as young as I used to be."

"Who is?"

He nodded. "I started thinking I was never going to get to that warm place if I didn't make a change soon. Then I got hired by Big Mac's Barbeque in Key Largo. They were failing and needed help. I took the job."

He smiled. "Then I happened to see an article about Mother's and The Palms and David in a local magazine a couple months back. I loved the idea of that kind of life so much that I decided to do something about it." He shrugged. "Here I am. If you don't want me, I totally understand that. Restaurant jobs are pretty easy to come by in Florida."

He looked around. "Not in a place like this, but I'll find something."

"This place is pretty special."

"I could tell that as soon as I got off the boat."

"This resort is more than my place of employment. It's my home. I'm an owner. I own part of the island, as well." He needed to know that if he was going to live and work here. Because he really was the right man for the job. Regardless of their past history, which was starting to feel less and less like something that mattered.

His brows went up. "You *have* done well for yourself."

"I was the recipient of a very generous gift. If you get this job, you will be, too. Being able to live here and work here is a once-in-a-lifetime opportunity."

He nodded, solemn. "That's exactly why I'm here."

Grace was glad he understood that, but she wasn't ready to give him the nod just yet. "I'll be in touch."

Chapter Nine

*L*eigh Ann went straight to Grant's studio from the family bungalows. It didn't take long, as they were closer to his studio than even the staff quarters. That got her wondering if full occupancy would affect him or not. The path from the marina to the family bungalows was new and would be getting a lot of use. It cut behind the outbuildings, angling into the island's interior, but kids were noisy.

Would the noise affect his ability to work? She hoped not. She hated to think he might have to look for a different studio. Having him on the island meant so much to her. He wasn't here every day. Some days he worked in his gallery, doing all the things necessary to keeping his business running.

But when he was in serious painting mode, like he was now, he was here.

She walked past the first two outbuildings. The

garage door that was the front wall of Grant's studio space was open.

She stepped inside, her eyes adjusting to the change in light, and saw a voluptuous young woman standing inches away from Grant, grinning up at him. Tiny blond braids covered her head, cascading down her back all the way to her hips, where they went pink for the last six inches. She was gesturing with one hand, twirling a few of those braids around a finger of the other.

She wore a hot pink full-length bodysuit with a white furry vest and white platform flipflops that elevated her petite frame at least four inches. Diamonds and gold flashed from her ears, neck, wrists, and fingers. Her only other accessory was a crossbody Chanel iPhone case in quilted white leather with a gold chain strap.

Lala Queen.

Leigh Ann stood there for a moment, taking it all in, not wanting to interrupt a guest, but at the same time feeling very much like Lala might be about to cross a boundary if she got one step closer to Grant.

Then Grant saw Leigh Ann and shot her a look that seemed to be a cry for assistance. That was all Leigh Ann needed. She went in, pasting on a cool, professional smile as she headed for Lala. "Hello there."

Grant exhaled in apparent relief and smiled.

"Hi—"

"Oh, hey, cool," Lala said. "I was wondering if there was service out here. Could you like, get me some water? Cold, obviously. Voss, if you have it. Or Fiji. And some lemons and limes. Slices, not wedges."

Leigh Ann was aware that in her tropical shirt and tan shorts, she looked like a resort employee. She was, *technically*, a resort employee. But she wasn't about to fetch water for Lala. She would, however, call the front desk and have some sent. Just as soon as she watched a few more moments of this interesting interaction.

"Anyway," Lala said as she turned back to Grant. "I totally want to be a mermaid, but with, like, a pink tail because pink is my vibe, you get it?"

Grant's hand came up to press against his temple. "Ms. Queen, as I explained, I am not a portrait artist. I don't do paintings on request."

Her hands went to her hips. Her fingernails, which looked about two inches long, were painted in various shades of pink and accented with rhinestones and pearly white hearts. "Well, you're painting one right now, aren't you?"

"I am working on a painting of my own."

"But there's a woman in it. Just make her me."

"My muse doesn't work that way."

Lala glanced at Leigh Ann. "Are you going to get my water or, like, not?"

"I'd be happy to call the front desk and ask them to

send you some. Do you want it sent to your bungalow?"

Lala made a face. "No, I want it now. Here. Keep up."

Leigh Ann pulled out her phone and called the pool bar. She'd never run into anyone so entitled at the resort before. She supposed there was always a first time. It would undoubtedly not be the last.

"Mother's pool bar, the water's great. How can I help you?"

"Chauncey, this is Leigh Ann. I'm at Grant's studio. Can you have some bottled water and sliced lemons and limes sent over for Lala Queen?"

"You got it."

"Thanks." Leigh Ann stuck the phone back in her pocket. "The water is on its way." Then she walked over to Grant and gave him a kiss. "Nice to see you."

"You, too," he said, giving her a wink.

Lala's artfully penciled brows arched. "You two are a thing?" She smirked at Grant. "I see you, boo. Getting busy with the help. Get some."

Grant narrowed his eyes at Lala. "Leigh Ann is not the help. She's one of the owners. Of the *island*. She's also the manager of the fitness center and spa."

Lala put a hand to her generous chest and fluttered her lashes, which were so unnaturally thick and long Leigh Ann wasn't sure how she kept her eyes open. "My bad. No wonder you didn't want to get me water."

"It's fine," Leigh Ann said. "Your water is on the way." She'd give Grant an extra special thank-you later for setting Lala straight. "I trust you're enjoying your stay here so far?"

"Like, totally. My crew are scouting locations right now so we can start shooting the video tomorrow. One of them is having a look at some new bungalow? Whatevs. It's cool."

"What's the name of the song that the video is for?"

"*Summer Love*. It'll be dropping in March."

Leigh Ann nodded. "I hope it goes very well for you."

"Me, too, yo. Can I talk at you for a minute?"

Leigh Ann blinked. "Aren't we talking now?"

"I mean private like."

"Ah. Of course." Leigh Ann gestured toward the outside.

They walked together. Although Lala didn't so much walk as sway. Leigh Ann couldn't imagine how long it took the young woman to get ready in the morning, but then, she supposed Lala had a team for that.

They stopped on the path. A pair of dolphins swam past about ten yards out, their fins cutting through the blue water. Leigh Ann pointed. "Look. Some of the locals."

"That's crazy," Lala said. She stared, mouth open. The sun glinted off one of her teeth that was somehow covered in diamonds. "I didn't know you had sharks around here."

"Those are dolphins. But we do have sharks, mostly small ones, though."

"Dolphins bite, though, right?"

Leigh Ann wondered about the kind of childhood Lala had had. "They could, I guess, but dolphins are generally known for their kind and playful behavior. They've been known to help swimmers in need, even defending them from sharks on occasion."

"For real like?"

Leigh Ann nodded. "Very much for real."

"That is so cool. I should get some dolphins for my video. Which reminds me. Owen Monk lives on this joint, right?"

Leigh Ann took "joint" to mean the island. "He lives on the other end of Compass Key, yes."

"I would, like, *die* to get him in my video. Just a cameo would be totally cool. Do you have his number?"

It was programed into her phone, right after Katie's. "No, I'm sorry. He's a very private man." Leigh Ann changed the subject. "What did you want to speak to me about?"

"Oh, right, yeah." Lala waved her fingernails at the interior of the studio. "Listen, can you, like, make that guy paint me? You're his boss, right?"

"No, I'm not his boss. Grant Shoemaker is a world-renowned artist. He simply uses this space as his studio because the light is so spectacular out here."

Lala stomped both feet. Not much of a stomp, but a clear indication that she wasn't happy. "Come on, you gotta get him to do it. I need to be a mermaid. Like, my friends would die. How much do you think he would charge? Because money's not a problem."

Leigh Ann shook her head. "I can talk to him, but I don't believe there's any price. He paints what he's moved to paint."

A server, Miguel, showed up with a tray bearing two bottles of water, two glasses of ice, and two dishes of sliced lemons and limes. He presented it to Lala. "Your water, Ms. Queen."

She wrinkled her nose. "Yanno...I'd rather have a daiquiri." She looked at Leigh Ann. "Get him to say yes, okay? Cool. Bye." Then she flounced off, pulling out her phone, and giving it all her attention.

Leigh Ann frowned. "We'll take the water, Miguel. Thank you."

He looked after Lala. "I've heard she's hard to please. And very demanding." He made a face. "Sorry. I know I shouldn't talk about a guest like that, but—"

"Don't worry about it. You did nothing wrong."

"Thanks. I'll take these in."

As he went into the studio, she watched Lala. Maybe it was time to send out a little employee email about the proper care of difficult guests.

Chapter Ten

Amanda headed back to the front office after the girls finished up their tour. Everything in the new bungalows looked wonderful and things were on track with Phase II to be done approximately when it should be. Having Duke and his father, Jack, on board to help had been a very wise move. Jack had actually come out of semi-retirement to take on the job of general contractor.

She was so happy that he'd done that for them. Dixie, Duke's mom, had texted Amanda the next day to say how happy Jack was that Amanda had asked.

A win-win if ever there was one.

The subcontractors who'd been brought in were all locals and they all seemed to know both men, but Jack especially. His years of working in the construction business were paying off. At least for the resort.

What a great guy he was. It was no wonder Duke was so great himself. Mother's was lucky to have both of them. Although she felt like she was getting the best part of that deal. She smiled as she walked into the lobby. A couple was getting their photo taken in front of the big Christmas tree.

It was covered in shells, sea-life ornaments, white and turquoise garlands, and had a tree topper made of more shells in the shape of a star. All of it had come from the many storage boxes that had been unearthed in the big reorganization. More decorations adorned various parts of the lobby, all from the storage rooms, all ignored for quite a few years.

In fact, the decorations they'd found were all over the resort. Including the lights that wrapped the big palms on the way in. They'd even found a big stand-up Santa wearing a Hawaiian shirt. He lit up when plugged in. He was currently doing a shift greeting guests at the marina.

Carissa was on the phone but hung up as Amanda approached. "How was it?"

"Fantastic. I cannot wait to do the employee tours. You're going to be blown away."

Carissa grinned. "How did Iris like her surprise?"

"There were tears, as expected." Amanda laughed. "She loved it. How's it going here?"

"Good. Pretty calm." Carissa bit her lip, her eyes sparkling with excitement. "I just found out I won the lottery for the shared bungalow."

"Oh, that is fantastic news." One of the spaces in

each of the new employee bungalows was being drawn for among the current employees. The rest would be held back until it was determined if any of the new hires needed them. "Do you know who you'll be sharing with yet?"

She shook her head. "No, but it doesn't matter. I'm sure they'll be great."

"I'm really pleased for you."

"Thanks."

Amanda's ringtone went off. She pulled her phone out to see her sister's name on the screen. "Hi, Denise."

"Hi. What's it like spending Christmas with no snow on the ground?"

Amanda smiled as she walked around the counter to her office. "Pretty nice, actually. It's beautiful here. About mid-seventies, low humidity, blue skies. I don't mean to rub it in, but it's the definition of paradise right now."

"No, go ahead, rub it in. I can take it."

Amanda laughed. "How are things there?"

"Great."

"And Mother?"

Denise sighed. "Still herself."

Amanda had sent her estranged mother a Christmas card but hadn't held out any hope something as simple as a card would change anything. "I'm sorry."

"It's not your fault. But ever since the two of you fell

out, she's been more Militant Marge than ever. I think she blames herself for what happened between you two. As she should. But she'd never admit that, of course, but that's my take."

"Have you thought about talking to her?"

Denise snorted. "Because that went so well when you tried it?"

Amanda slipped back into the office. "I just thought maybe she'd be a little more receptive, seeing as how she's only on speaking terms with one of her children. Maybe that might wake her up a little."

"I don't think Mom will ever wake up."

So sad. "Does she ever mention me?"

"No. And whenever I say anything about you, she ignores it and changes the subject."

Amanda rolled her eyes. "She is so stubborn. I sent her a Christmas card. Fat lot of good that will do. She probably didn't even open it, just threw it in the trash." She sat down at the desk.

"That wouldn't surprise me. What are you doing for Christmas?"

"I'm going to FaceTime with Wyatt and Shelby in the morning, then later on Duke and I are going to his parents' house for Christmas dinner. His sister will be there. I'm looking forward to it."

"I bet you are. I'm sure it'll be great."

"What are you doing?"

"As I'm sure you already know, Wyatt and Renee are coming here."

"I did know that."

"Mom is insisting we all go to the country club for Christmas brunch. All I can say is I hope the punch is spiked. After that, we're just coming back to my house and enjoying the day."

"When are you coming to visit?" Amanda had been trying to get her sister to Compass Key for a while.

"Soon. I mean it. I'm sorry things haven't worked out to make that happen already. How about January? I can get a week off from work."

It would be a busy time of year for the resort, especially with all the new construction going on, but Amanda wasn't going to let that stand in the way. "Sounds good to me. Whenever you can get here is great. My schedule is probably more flexible than yours. I just really want to see you. And for you to see this place."

"And," Denise added. "I really want to meet Duke."

Amanda grinned. "I know you do. I want you to meet him, too." The idea still made her a little nervous, but not nearly as much as it had in the beginning. "Although I was thinking that if you and Shelby could coordinate your visits, that would be even better."

Denise let out a happy gasp. "Then I could finally meet my grand-nephew in person."

Amanda smiled. Shelby had given birth to healthy

baby boy almost three months ago, Noah. So far, Amanda had only seen her first grandchild in pictures and on FaceTime. "That's what I was thinking. I want to hold that baby so badly I can't even tell you."

"I'll talk to Shelby about her schedule soon. Do you think Jacob will come with her?"

"I don't know. His schedule is pretty hectic. But I have a guest room and a pull-out couch, so there's room for whoever comes. And I can borrow a crib from housekeeping."

"We will make this happen," Denise said. "I promise."

"You know, that's really all the Christmas gift I need."

"I love you, sis."

"I love you, too. Best of luck with Mom."

Denise laughed. "Thanks. Talk to you soon. Merry Christmas."

"Merry Christmas." Amanda hung up. She regretted nothing about moving her life to Compass Key, but she did miss her family. Funny that it had taken such a drastic change in her life to get closer to them but moving here had made her take a hard look at who she was and how she'd treated people.

Duke had helped a lot with that, too.

Which reminded her that she still had no present for him and no idea what to get him. She picked up her phone again and dialed his mom, Dixie.

If there was anyone who could give Amanda some guidance on what to buy for Duke, it had to be his mom.

And if she didn't have any ideas, Amanda would go find Jack and ask him. One of them had to be able to help her.

Chapter Eleven

Katie was absolutely excited about writing her new series. But knowing her son was only hours away was proving to be a bigger distraction than she could overcome. She'd written and rewritten the last paragraph so many times she no longer knew what it said. Or was supposed to say.

So when her phone rang, she was more than happy to answer it, something she generally didn't do when she was in writing mode. Although it was Owen. Talking to him was always a nice break.

She answered with a big smile on her face. "Hello, fiancé."

He laughed as he always did when she greeted him that way. "How's the queen of romance?"

"Eh." Katie snorted. "I've had better writing days. My head would rather focus on Josh and his family arriving than Kalema Island."

"I'd say I was sorry you're having trouble with your word count, except I was about to interrupt it anyway."

"You were? Why?" She hit Save so that she wouldn't lose the little bit of writing she had accomplished.

"Well..." He drew the word out in such a way that she knew he was up to something. "Your Christmas present was delivered early. Which I'm happy about. But that means you're getting it early, too. I hope you're okay with that."

She grinned. She was pretty pleased with the gift she'd gotten him. It was a picture of his beloved cat, Hisstopher, made up like an English lord. Buying for a billionaire wasn't easy. "If this is a play to get yours early, it's not going to work. I mean, nice try, but uh-uh."

He laughed. "No, no, I can wait. But yours can't. If you're able to break away, can you meet me at your end of the boardwalk in about three minutes?"

"How about five?"

"That works. See you then."

She hung up, then ran to the bedroom to put on something cuter than the old T-shirt and bleach-stained yoga pants she was currently dressed in. She went with capri jeans and a dressier top that tied at the waist. Then she brushed her teeth and hair, slicked on some mascara and lip gloss, grabbed her phone and headed for the door. "Soph! I'm running out for a minute to meet Owen. Back in a bit."

"Okay," Sophie yelled back. "Have fun."

Katie went through the door between the two sets of interior stairs, then took the outside steps down to the ground level. She wasn't sure where she was at on the five minutes, but she saw Owen leaning on the railing at the start of the boardwalk when she rounded the corner.

He smiled when he saw her. "Hi there."

"Hi. Were you waiting long?"

He shook his head. "Nope. Thanks for meeting me."

"Thanks for giving me a valid reason to procrastinate."

Still smiling, he reached into his back pocket and pulled out a blue bandana folded lengthwise. "Sorry, but you're going to have to be blindfolded for this next part."

"What?" She narrowed her eyes. "What kind of gift is this?"

"You'll see. Eventually." He held up the blindfold. "Ready?"

"I guess." She turned around and closed her eyes.

He put the blindfold on her. "Is that okay?"

She adjusted it slightly. "Yep."

He tied it, then took her hand. "You can't see, right?"

"Nope."

"Good." He took her by the shoulders. "Now I'm going to turn you around three times."

"Hang on." But he'd already started spinning her. Thankfully, he didn't let go.

He took her hand and she grabbed for it, holding onto his arm. "Okay, walk forward."

"Easier said than done."

"I won't let you go."

"You'd better not. I don't want to spend Christmas in the hospital."

"I won't let you fall."

There was so much happiness in his voice that she just went with it. She couldn't imagine what his gift might be and all the setup was only confusing her more. They started walking. In a few short steps the ground beneath them changed from the smoothness of the boardwalk to the crunchy softness of the sandy path.

There were no smells or sounds to give her any clues, because most of the island smelled and sounded the same way. Tropical flowers, fresh air, and the almost ever-present lapping of the water, along with an occasional bird cry or overheard conversation.

The ground changed again, back to hard, smooth boards. Were they on the boardwalk again? They must be. He must have led her off then back on to further confuse her. He was so tricky.

"Okay, here we are." He brought them to a stop.

She felt him untie the blindfold. She blinked when it came off. They were standing on the dock at Arthur's Marina. She shook her head. "I don't know what I'm looking at."

Owen pointed. "Right there."

He was directing her to look at a sleek black and white pontoon boat that looked brand new. Then she saw the big red bow on the front of it.

Her mouth came open.

He kissed her cheek. "Merry Christmas, sweetheart."

She stared in silence for another second or two before looking at him. "You didn't really buy me a boat, did you?"

He nodded. "Top of the line Sylan pontoon. Twenty-eight feet. Three-hundred and fifty horse-power, with a top speed of fifty-two miles an hour, which is probably faster than you will ever go in it, but this baby can move. You could ski behind it." He shrugged. "Or, you know, drive it at a reasonable speed to my house."

She laughed. "You bought me a boat. You're crazy."

"About you."

She grabbed his face and kissed him, wrapping her arms around him.

"I just figured with your son and his family coming,

this might be the right time for you to have your own boat."

"But I don't know how to drive it. I don't think I'm even allowed, am I? I need some kind of license or something, right? At least insurance."

"Insurance is taken care of. It's in my name right now with you as an additional driver, but we can transfer it to you in the next couple of days. And you already took the boater safety course."

Katie nodded. "The one Iris made us all take." Iris had insisted on it, saying that if they were going to live on an island, they needed to know the basics about boat safety.

"Yes. So you have that card, and you were born before January 1st of 1988—"

"Thanks for the reminder that I'm old."

He grinned. "I'm just saying you're good to go. And I can teach you to drive. It's really easy. A boat like this is a joy to handle."

It was pretty exciting to think that was her boat.

He put his hand on her hip. "What do you say?"

"I say let me get my sunglasses and a hat and I'm all yours." The writing could be done later. Like next week. Putting off work wasn't optimal, but it was Christmas week, her son was about to arrive, and her fiancé had just bought her a boat. If there was ever a time to make an exception, this was it.

"Go on then. I'll be right here."

Katie raced back upstairs and into the house, which took her into the combined living room, dining room and kitchen area. Sophie was sitting on the couch, headphones on, and looked deep in the midst of something. Fabio was sleeping on the cushion next to her.

Katie went to her bedroom and got her sunglasses and a ballcap, then put her hair in a ponytail and slipped the hat on, adjusting it so it wouldn't fly off.

Although she didn't imagine they'd be going too fast. Not while she was learning to drive.

She went back out to the living room. Sophie looked up, pushing her headphones back. "Are you going out again?"

Katie grinned, unable to do anything else with her face. "Owen bought me a boat for Christmas. He's going to show me how to drive it."

Sophie's brows shot up. "A boat? Seriously?"

Katie nodded. "It's beautiful. A pontoon."

"Wow. Have fun. And tell him I said thanks, because now you can take me grocery shopping."

Katie laughed. "I'll let him know."

She ran back down and joined Owen, who was already on the boat. He gave her a hand getting on board. The pontoon was gorgeous, with sleek leather seats and a Bimini top that would give her all kinds of shade on hot days. It even had two motors on the back, which Katie didn't know a whole lot about but two seemed better than one. "This is amazing. I can't believe you did this. Except that I can, because you are the most wonderful, generous man I've ever known. Thank you."

"You're welcome." Then he winked at her. "Just remember that when I'm teaching you how to dock."

Chapter Twelve

*O*livia ran through her daily checklist of things to do, but everything on it was already done. She'd known that, she just couldn't help but look over it one more time before she called it quits for the day. Sometimes, she felt guilty about ending her day before five, but she started early. And sometimes, there was only so much accounting that could be done.

Christmas bonuses had been sent out the first week of December so that employees could use the money for gifts or anything else they might need. All of them, Olivia was happy to see, had been cashed already.

Not that she thought any of the bonuses would be ignored. It was just good to have the accounts settled in a timely fashion.

She straightened her desk, turned off her computer, then locked the door behind her as she left. Her Christmas shopping was done. She'd gotten Eddie a new coffeemaker and a supply of Cuban coffee. His current coffeemaker wasn't in great shape. It no longer heated the water quite as hot as Eddie liked it and the pot had a chipped handle. The one she'd bought him made espresso, which meant it could make Cuban-style coffee.

After extensive research, she'd *also* gotten him a gorgeous marine watch that had GPS, a tide tracker, a thermometer, and all kinds of other features that were supposed to be perfect for the enthusiastic boater. It hadn't been cheap, but she would have spent twice as much to get him something that seemed so perfect for him.

To make it extra special, she'd had the back engraved, *With Love, Olivia 12.25.22*. She couldn't wait to give it to him.

For Jenny, she'd bought a beautiful pair of earrings made from sea glass along with a matching bracelet.

For Leigh Ann, Amanda, Grace, and Katie, Olivia had ordered lovely turquoise rain jackets emblazoned with "Mother's Resort" on the front chest. She'd ordered one for Iris and Eddie, too, but theirs were in deep sea blue. She'd gotten one sent to her by an imprinting company looking for business and she'd liked it so much, they'd gotten a sale.

If the jackets were a really big hit, she was thinking it could be an item to carry in the boutique. It rained a lot in Florida, but most visitors never thought to bring a jacket for protection. Even she hadn't realized how often it rained until she'd moved here.

She walked slowly so she could take a good look at everything around her and make sure nothing needed attention.

Maybe a rain jacket was too practical of a gift, but Olivia didn't see anything wrong with practical presents. Better than stuff that just sat around collecting dust or didn't get used because it wasn't to the recipient's taste.

Although she imagined it was possible no one would like these jackets, either. Well, if they didn't, there was an island full of employees who'd probably be happy to take them. She picked up an empty water bottle from the ground and put it in the nearest recycling bin.

As far as what Eddie might be getting her, she had no idea and didn't care, because she would love it no matter what it was. The very idea that for the first time in quite a few years she would not be spending Christmas alone was really all the gift she needed.

Not just because she and Eddie would be together, but because Jenny would be with her, too. Jenny and Nick and all the girls and their guys. In less than a year, Olivia's life had gone from a rather sad, lonely existence to one overflowing with family, which was what she considered all of those people.

She sniffed. It made her emotional to be so overwhelmed with the blessing of this place. Even better, Eddie was coming over for dinner tonight. She wasn't making anything all that exciting. London broil, broccoli with cheese sauce and salad. Eddie, who loved carbs in a way that threatened Olivia's waistline, had insisted on bringing dessert.

She didn't know what it would be, but she'd learned months ago that Eddie's desserts were all sinfully good and not even remotely on her diet.

He loved to tell her she didn't need to lose weight and he loved her just the way she was, but since she'd been cutting back on carbs and swimming laps three times a week, she'd dropped fifteen pounds and he hadn't complained about that.

Or her new hair. She'd started going to the resort's salon and now wore her hair in an easy shag that made the most of its natural body. She got highlights, too, and the blond streaks made the existing gray practically disappear.

Even Jenny had complimented her personal makeover. Always nice to hear encouraging words from her daughter. Olivia knew Jenny paid attention to things like fashion and trends. It was sort of her job to know that stuff. Hard to run someone's social media in a successful way otherwise.

Olivia turned down the path that led to the employee bungalows.

From what Katie and Sophie had to say, Jenny was

doing a tremendous job with Katie's social media. Katie, as Iris Deveraux, wrote very sexy romances, although she'd already announced her new series was going to focus more on the romances and less on what happened between the sheets.

Olivia paused in front of the new employee bungalows. She could hear movement inside and knew the men would still be at work. She looked at her watch. Almost four, though. They'd be knocking off anytime now.

She went up the steps of one of the big bungalows to see how it was going.

Jack Shaw greeted her as she came through the door. "Hey there."

"Hi, Jack. You don't mind if I have a look around, do you?"

"Help yourself, Livie."

She smiled. No one had called her that since college, but she didn't mind. Jack said it with such affection there was no way it could bother her. "Thanks."

Unlike her bungalow with one bedroom up and one bedroom down, this had two up and two down, along with separate bathrooms for each one. The living room-dining room space wasn't as deep, but it was wider, so still plenty roomy. The kitchens were a little different, as well. They still had a breakfast bar that could handle a row of stools, but these kitchens were big enough to have an island, which meant more storage.

The bungalow had the same pantry with a washer and dryer, too, although none of the appliances were in yet.

Jack caught her looking into the empty laundry closet. "Appliances will be here after the new year."

She nodded. "Just about done, huh?"

"Yep. We should have the CO's by the end of January."

She'd learned enough to know that meant Certificate of Occupancy. "That's great. It's all coming together."

"It sure is."

She wandered on through, admiring the driftwood-colored plank vinyl that was already installed. It honestly looked like wood but would wear like concrete. Jack had recommended it. He'd helped them do a lot of the design work, actually, suggesting products that would have a long life while still looking good.

Whoever ended up living here should be very happy.

She gave Jack a wave and went on to her place. Eddie wouldn't be over for dinner until six-thirty, which meant she had plenty of time to swim some laps. The pool, thankfully, was heated to eighty-eight degrees this time of year — all through solar power, which she liked, because it was definitely energy efficient.

Owen was currently working on some new solar power ideas for electricity, too. She'd made him promise that the employee bungalows could be a test area if he got that far.

Anything she could do to save the resort money while also making things better put a smile on her face. Not as much as Eddie, but close.

She swam her laps, got a shower, then started to prep for dinner. She put on one of her favorite "shows" for this time of year, a crackling fireplace with a sound-track of Christmas music.

Eddie showed up at six-twenty-five, his hair still damp from the shower he'd taken. He smelled like lime and spices and looked like all kinds of wonderful to her. She'd left the door open for him, so he joined her in the kitchen, put a foil-covered baking dish on the counter, then wrapped his arms around her waist and kissed her cheek.

She stared at him. "I hate to tell you this, but you look tired."

"I am, *mamacita*. I don't think I've ever made so many trips as I have in these past couple of weeks."

His term of endearment for her almost made her smile but seeing him so worn out made smiling impos-sible. "We're hiring another boat captain."

He frowned. "I thought that had to be voted on."

She shook her head. "Not anymore. Iris even suggested we hire someone. As of now, it's a done deal. We just need to find the right person. And when Phase II opens, we'll bring on another part-timer if need be. In fact, I'll send out an email about it first thing in the morning. You and Rico are being run ragged."

"It's too bad Luis didn't work out."

She nodded. "It is." Luis had been a part-time captain, brought in to help ferry the construction crews, tools, and supplies to the island, but he'd never returned after Thanksgiving. He'd just disappeared on them, leaving them high and dry. "Do you have any ideas?"

"No, but I can ask at Bluewater. They might know a few possible candidates."

"Good. That would be great."

He smiled. "Thank you." He kissed her again. "I like these special privileges."

She laughed. "Doing what's best for the resort and its employees isn't a special privilege."

He shrugged, amusement sparkling in his eyes. "Whatever you want to call it is fine by me." He patted the dish he'd brought. "I'm very happy I made these. You've definitely earned them."

She eyed the dish. "What is it?"

"Guava bars." He pulled off the foil to reveal the treat inside.

The cut squares had a crumbly topping through

which she could see a deep red jelly layer. The smell was sweet and tangy and made her mouth water. She'd come to love the taste of guava since living here.

She shot him a look. "Those do not look low-carb."

"*Mamacita*," he said, pulling her close. "You are skinny enough already."

Chapter Thirteen

At the sound of Nick walking in the door, Jenny looked up. "Is it really dark outside already?"

He nodded. "Been that way for a while."

She leaned back from the computer and stretched. "I just lost track of time. How was your day?"

"Busy. I had a jellyfish sting, a splinter, a sea urchin puncture, a couple of sunburns, one of the line cooks cut his finger badly enough to require stiches, and to top it all off, an allergic reaction to mango."

"Mango?"

He nodded. "It's more about the skin of the fruit than the flesh. It's more common than you'd think." He sat across from her, toed off his shoes, and put his feet up. "How was your day?"

"Busy, too, but not nearly that exciting. I'm creating a graphics portfolio for Katie's new series so I can start to build buzz and preorders as soon as that first cover goes up." She exhaled, smiling at him. Such a nice face to end the day with.

"You hungry?"

"Starving, actually." She let out a little moan of self-pity, because the idea of having to cook did not appeal. "I can't wait until Castaways is open."

He laughed. "I bet I can guess why in three words." He paused, then said, "Brick oven pizza."

"Heck, yes." She grinned. "And open until 2 a.m. during high season? I honestly might never have to leave here again."

"We have that pizza dough in a can stuff. I'm pretty sure I could handle making that."

"Yeah? Because if so, that would officially qualify you for the Best Boyfriend In The World award and I hear competition is pretty steep this time of year."

He stood up. "I'm on it."

"My hero."

His smile held on a few more seconds before fading. "I have something to tell you. I didn't want to tell you by text or a phone call and I've been trying to come up with the right words all day, but I'm not sure there are any."

She sat up, suddenly worried about what he was going to say. "Are you breaking up with me? Is us living together not working out? Because I swear, I can be neater."

"What?" He snorted. "No. You are plenty neat. And I love you being here." He sighed. "My mother is coming to visit tomorrow. And she's going to be staying here."

Jenny didn't say anything for a minute. Just sat there and considered what he'd said. "Do you want me to stay with my mom while she's here? Would that be easier?"

He laughed but there was no joy in the sound. "Easier for you? Definitely. And if that's what you want to do, I completely understand."

She stood up. "What do you want me to do?"

"I want you here. But that's a selfish answer. My mother is...well, you know what I've told you about her. She's all of that. And probably more. And I have no idea how she'll react to you."

He exhaled loudly and stared at the ceiling for a second. "That's a lie. I have a great idea of how she'll react to you. You won't be good enough. She'll find fault in everything you do. Your job. The way you dress. How she perceives your treatment of me. All of it."

Jenny wasn't looking forward to that.

He frowned. "Maybe you should go to your mom's."

"Why is your mother coming so suddenly?"

"She insisted on seeing me or she threatened to make trouble. I talked to Iris about it, and she said let her come."

Jenny could see the regret and concern on his face. This was tormenting him. "Maybe she won't be like that."

"It's sweet of you to want to give her the benefit of the doubt but trust me. She'll be everything I said and worse."

"Even at Christmas?"

"Yep."

She put her arms around him. "We could just kill her with kindness. Metaphorically speaking, of course."

He kissed the top of her head. "I love that you want to try. I'm just worried you'll hate her so much you'll want nothing to do with me."

"Hey." She looked up at him. "I'm not that shallow."

He smiled again. "No, you're not. But you've yet to meet her and she is a force to be reckoned with. When she doesn't like something or someone, she will wage an all-out war."

"You forget what I do for a living. I find the silver lining in bad situations. I get people out of all kinds of bad press, giving terrible situations the best possible outcomes." She grinned at him as she realized she was precisely the woman for this job. "Maybe I'm exactly what your mother needs."

"What she needs is solitary confinement. But if you're willing to take a crack at getting to know her, I will be eternally in your debt."

She gave him a wink. "Make me a pizza and we're even."

He laughed his maniacal cartoon-villain laugh that always cracked her up. "You're so easy."

"Not so fast. I want extra cheese."

He went to the fridge and started pulling out ingredients. "Hey, we have a bag of pepperoni. You want me to put those on it, too?"

"Yes."

"Hot peppers?"

"No. Well, maybe a few."

He held up a small plastic container. "What are these?"

"Chopped red onion left over from the tuna salad I made the other day. Yes."

"Grapes?"

She laughed. "*No.*"

He held up a jar. "These things?"

"Pickles?" She loved it when he was silly. It was such a rare quality in most guys. "Nope. Cheese, pepperoni, and onion. That's plenty."

He got out a cookie sheet, opened the roll of pizza dough, and went to work stretching it out on the sheet.

Jenny didn't honestly know how his mother's visit would go, but she wasn't about to let him face her alone. Jenny was too worried his mother might try to turn Nick against her if given the chance.

The best thing Jenny could do was glue herself to

his side and be the best girlfriend she could be so that Yolanda had no reason to convince him otherwise.

Chapter Fourteen

Grace sat on a stool in The Palm's kitchen at the end of the hot line while David worked. It wasn't ideal but it was the only way to talk to him sometimes. And she'd leave before the dinner rush. He was mostly just doing some prep now, which meant he could still carry on a conversation that had nothing to do with which ticket was up next.

She explained her conversation with Curt to him, doing her best not to leave out any details. "So what do you think?"

"I think he's a great candidate and probably overqualified for the job, but this doesn't feel like my decision to make. It's yours. You have to be all right with him not just working for you, but living in this very small community with you. There won't be any way to avoid him if something goes wrong."

"No. But we could always fire him if it's that big of a deal."

David looked up from the work he was doing. "We could. But do you really want to hire someone with that as your backup plan?"

"Isn't that the backup plan for every employee we bring on?"

"Yes, but it's generally not because my wife was once engaged to them."

She sighed. "I understand what you're saying. I don't foresee there being any problem. I have no feelings of any kind toward him, and it seems he's moved on, too."

David adjusted his grip on his knife. "It *seems* he's moved on?"

"I have no reason to think he feels anything but sorry."

David thought for a moment. "What if we hire him on a probationary basis? That way he knows his circumstances could change and he'll be on his best behavior. Or...we don't hire him at all."

Grace couldn't help but feel bad that the resort would miss out on someone as qualified as Curt. Or that Curt might not get a job this good because of their past, which was starting more and more to seem like a non-issue. "I think the probationary basis is a great solution."

"Works for me," David said. "Any other potential hires from the interviews today?"

"Three, actually. One is another of the resumes you gave me. Jamarcus Mullins?"

David nodded. "The line cook. You were his second interview."

"Right and I thought he was great. Young, seems eager, great food knowledge. Pizza oven experience, which I'm sure was part of why you pulled his resume. Anyway, he should be a definite."

"Call him and tell him. Will he be able to get staff accommodations? Because if he's going to be working the late shift, it might be easier for him to just be here."

"I don't see why not." She smiled. It was always fun to make the call telling someone they'd gotten the job.

"Great. Who's next?"

"The second is a young woman, Taylor Fredericks. She's a little bit of a hippie chick, but very sweet with a bubbly personality that would be great for front of the house. I'd like to bring her on as a server. She's only ever worked at an Applebee's, but I can train her. And she won't need housing because she lives ten minutes from Bluewater Marina, so she can be ferried in. Plus, she's apparently fluent in ASL."

"Always good if we have some hearing-impaired guests. I'm good with that choice. Who else?"

"Last one is another wait staff pick. Enrique Hernandez. Clean cut, super well-mannered, speaks English, Spanish, and Portuguese. Has nearly ten years of experience that includes cruise ship work and fine dining. I don't know his housing situation, but he mentioned getting together with his mother and sister for Sunday dinners, so it didn't seem like he'd need accommodations but I'll ask."

"Great picks. I'm good with all of them."

"Awesome." She closed the file she'd been balancing on her knees. "I'll make the calls."

"Does that include Curt?"

She nodded. "Yes. You're still good with that?"

"I am. So long as you are. I told you, this is up to you."

"Then I think he's a great choice. You need someone who can be your right-hand man and keep an eye on these restaurants when you can't be there. I believe Curt is that guy. We certainly haven't interviewed anyone else with that much experience."

"All right. Make your calls." One side of his mouth hitched up in a lopsided grin. "I never thought I'd be working with your ex-fiancé."

"And I'm sure he never thought he'd be working for me and my husband. It'll be fine." More and more tickets were starting to come in. It was time for her to go. "I'm off to make those calls. See you tonight?"

"See you tonight. Love you."

She smiled as she hopped off the stool. "Love you, too."

She walked through the kitchen, making sure to say hi to Chantelle on her way out. As Grace left, a few servers were coming in through the other door. Definitely time to go.

She took her time walking back to the bungalow, thinking about what it would be like to live and work in the same vicinity as Curt. Since she'd talked to him and he'd explained things, she really didn't have any bad feelings about him or him being here.

Leigh Ann was standing outside talking to Amanda, so Grace went over to say hi.

Amanda waved. "How did it go today?"

"Good," Grace said as she joined them. "We've got four new hires. I'm about to call them and let them know."

Leigh Ann smiled. "But that does not include your ex, right?"

"As a matter of fact," Grace said. "It does. I called him back and we had a long talk. He explained what happened, which was that he basically had a mental breakdown about school and marrying me and all the responsibility that entailed."

"So that's why he disappeared on you?"

Grace nodded. "Yep. He was really apologetic. And we're hiring him because he's got years of experience running restaurants. Saving them, actually. He's been working as a restaurant rehabilitator."

"Meaning what exactly?" Amanda asked.

"He goes into failing restaurants, fixes what's wrong, and turns them around to make them profitable again. Granted, that's not the issue here, but anyone who can do that can run a restaurant no problem."

"Hmm." Amanda tipped her head. "Sounds like he'd be able to spot problems before they happen, too."

"I should think so." Grace got her key out. "Anyway, I'm off to call the new hires and tell them the good news. One of them will most likely be taking a room in the shared bungalow. I'll email about the new hires once they're all confirmed."

"That reminds me," Amanda said. "Carissa at the front desk won the lottery for one of the rooms."

"Good for her," Grace said. "All right, see you guys later."

Leigh Ann put her hand on Grace's arm. "Before you go, I was just telling Amanda about the little run-in I had with Lala Queen today."

"Run-in?" Grace made a face. "You make it sound like there was a fight."

"Not a fight." Leigh Ann explained what had happened. "I just wanted to give you guys the heads-up about her. I'm going to send out an email to the employee loop, letting them know she might require some extra finessing. I'll send you guys the email first so you can look it over. I'd be happy for any input."

"Sure," Amanda said. "But isn't that Katie's job? She's the communications director."

"She is, you're right, but her son gets in tonight. I hate to bother her."

"Bother her," Grace said. "Writing is her thing, and she can easily look it over on her phone. Won't take but a couple minutes. And if you don't get her input, she'll feel bad."

Leigh Ann nodded. "You're right. I'll text her to let her know what's up."

"Great." Grace gave her friends a little wave. "Have a good night."

She went off to her bungalow, let herself in, and went straight to the couch with her phone and her file of resumes.

She called Jamarcus, Taylor, and Enrique in quick succession, confirming that Jamarcus would very much like accommodations. It only made sense, especially if he was going to work as late as 2 a.m. during the busy months.

Being slightly isolated on Compass Key was both an advantage and a disadvantage but having onsite staff housing helped a lot.

She looked at the last resume. Curt. She dialed his number.

"Hello?"

"Curt, it's Grace."

"Hey. I wasn't expecting to hear back from you today."

"Well, we've made our decision and we'd like to offer you the job on a probationary basis."

"Really?" He seemed genuinely surprised. "I did not see that coming. I thought because of our past…"

He didn't need to finish his thought. She understood. "Let's think of this as a fresh start, okay? Leave the past in the past and move forward without any of that baggage."

"I'd like that very much. Thank you. I really mean that."

"I'll be in touch soon to give you a move-in date and I'm sure David will contact you about when training will begin. Although you probably won't need that much. Mostly there will be some resort things you'll need to learn, the history of the place, some of that kind of stuff."

"Great. Looking forward to it."

She smiled. "Have a good night. We'll talk to you soon."

"You, too. Thanks again." He hung up.

She put her phone down and took a breath. All of her calls had gone well. Things were moving in the right direction.

Now they just needed to stay that way.

Chapter Fifteen

*L*eigh Ann opened the door and grinned at the man on her front porch. "Hi there."

"Hello, beautiful." Grant stepped inside, took her in his arms, and kissed her. "I missed you."

She pushed the door shut. "You just saw me a couple hours ago."

"Was that all it was? Seems like *ages*."

She laughed. "How was the rest of your day?"

"Not as productive as I would have liked, but tomorrow is another day."

She tucked a strand of hair behind her ear as he released her. "Please tell me Lala didn't come back."

"She did, just for a few minutes." He let out a long sigh. "I don't want to get a guest into trouble, but that one is a handful. She doesn't take no for an answer. And she disrupted my flow."

"That's really not acceptable." Leigh Ann crossed her arms, truly bothered that Lala, a guest, was overstepping her bounds. Clearly, Lala was a woman used to getting her own way. But there were limits to everything. "Katie helped me work up an email that I just sent out to the employee loop letting them know that there was a guest on the property that might need more careful handling and extra attention, but that if anyone felt that guest crossed a line with them, they were to report it immediately."

He shrugged. "But what can you do? I can't imagine how much she's spent to bring her whole team here for this video. Plus the equipment. She's got to have a serious amount of cash tied up in it."

"Which is exactly why she should be behaving better. We reserve the right to dismiss any guest who becomes a nuisance." She moved her hands to her hips and rolled her eyes. "Except that we really don't need that kind of publicity right now."

"Because of Phase II?"

"Exactly." She went back into the kitchen where she'd been working on dinner. Broiled salmon, wild rice, and a cold roasted Brussels sprouts salad with balsamic vinegar and slivered almonds.

Grant followed. "What can I do to help?"

She checked on the salmon, then turned around. "Paint her picture?"

"I meant with dinner."

Leigh Ann chuckled softly. "The table's set, food's about ready. You could open that bottle of wine and pour me a glass. Although it would help if you painted her picture."

"You know I can't do that."

She leaned against the counter, suddenly curious. "I don't think I do. In all seriousness, why can't you?"

"Because then I'd have to do it for every other request that came along. It's not what I do."

"I understand that, but if you charge her an outrageous fee, there won't be any other requests. Or very few, anyway. I realize this resort gets its share of the uber wealthy who can afford such things, but I think those who'd want to be painted would be pretty rare."

He seemed unconvinced. "I don't know."

"What did you sell *The Goddess of the Eagle Rays* for?" That was the first picture he'd painted where she'd been his muse. He'd put her front and center. The painting's reception had been stellar.

He glanced at her. "Two hundred and fifty thousand."

Leigh Ann shrugged. "So tell Lala that's your price for an original piece of artwork. Or tell her three, if that sounds better. Or some other big number. But I bet that shuts her up. I bet she doesn't go through with it."

He pulled the cork out of the bottle. "And if she does?"

"Then you paint her as a pink mermaid and call it a day." The timer went off on the salmon. She put on an oven mitt and pulled the fish out, setting the pan on the stovetop. "Maybe she'll forget about it tomorrow. Maybe it was a whim and it's over."

"Let's hope so."

"Would it really be the worst thing to paint her? Think about all the social media attention you'd get."

He poured a glass of wine for each of them. "That's part of what worries me. My gallery isn't equipped to handle a sudden influx like that."

She dished up the wild rice and carried it and the Brussels sprouts salad to the table. "Then you hire some temporary help." She straightened and put her hand on his chest. "Look, I know you paint as you're moved to do so. I know you're not about over-commercializing your work. I love all of that and I would never try to change you. But you *are* running a business. And sometimes, you have to make compromises. I just don't think this compromise would have any lasting downside. And the potential for good benefits is much more likely."

He nodded. "You're probably right. Maybe I'm being too stubborn about it."

She smiled. "You're one of the easiest-going guys I know. It's okay to be stubborn or passionate or whatever you want to call it about your work. It's art. That kind of creativity comes with its own set of rules. Lala should understand that more than anyone."

"Assuming what she does can actually be called art."

Leigh Ann snorted as she went back to the kitchen for the salmon. "At the very least, I'd think she considers herself creative. Maybe you can appeal to that side of her sensibilities. Although I tend to think that for the right amount of money, she'd write or perform a song for just about anyone."

He nodded. "Probably a safe guess. Dinner looks great, by the way. How about a walk on the beach after?"

"That sounds lovely." The temperature had dipped into the mid-sixties, but Leigh Ann loved it. She knew this brief time of year was the only chance to enjoy the cooler temps, so she was more than happy to be out in them. So long as it wasn't rainy, which it wasn't.

So after dinner, that's exactly what they did. Leigh Ann put on jeans and a sweatshirt along with some slip-on sneakers. Grant put on a light jacket over his denim shirt and jeans, but stayed in his flipflops.

Men, she thought, never seemed to feel the cold like women did.

They strolled hand in hand, mostly silent, along the length of the beach. There were others out doing the same thing. It was a beautiful night for it, the sky was full of stars that seemed so bright and beautiful, it was like even the heavens knew Christmas was coming.

And maybe they did.

They stopped to watch a falling star. Grant put his arm around her. When they started walking again, a cloud of pink was headed toward them.

"Yoo-hoo!" Lala Queen waved like she was signaling for a plane to land.

Like there was any chance they might not see her.

"Good evening, Ms. Queen," Grant said.

"Hello, Mr. Painter Man." She grinned from under the froth of an enormous hooded coat constructed of pink fake fur and possibly feathers. A bodyguard in a black track suit trailed her. "So are you going to paint me or what?"

Grant took a breath. "Ms. Queen—"

"Call me Lala, please."

"Lala, we haven't even discussed price."

She shrugged. "So. Holler at me."

"My last original piece sold for a quarter of a million. And that wasn't custom."

"All right. So what do you want? Double? I want a big painting. Something impressive, you feel me?"

Grant glanced at Leigh Ann, but this was his business and she wasn't going to say anything more. He had to decide what he was going to do.

He looked at Lala again. "Why don't you give me your number and I'll text you in the morning with my final price once I consider the work in its entirety."

To Leigh Ann that sounded like a stall technique.

Lala just held out her hand, her long nails gleaming like talons. "Give me your phone and I'll punch in my digits."

He handed over his phone.

She used the pad of her finger to add her number to his contacts. "There you go. Don't call too early."

Grant nodded. "Right."

Lala went on her way.

Grant looked at Leigh Ann. "I can't believe I'm going to do this."

"I can't believe how much she's willing to pay."

He shook his head. "That's the only reason I'm doing it. My boat needs to be revarnished and I do not want to do it myself, but it's not cheap to have it done right. Might as well let Lala pay for that."

She smiled. "And if you just happen to sell more prints in the process, it's all good."

"It better be."

"It will be." She hooked her arm through his and got them moving again. "My boyfriend, the celebrity portrait painter. So long as you want to be a mermaid."

Chapter Sixteen

*A*manda stared at the row of stores ahead of her. She had an hour left before she had to be back at Bluewater Marina to get a ride to the island and she still had no present for Duke. And that was after two hours of looking already.

Talking to his mom had been nice, but Dixie hadn't been able to come up with any ideas about what to get him either. She'd confessed to Amanda that she'd resorted to a book about architecture and a nice T-shirt.

Amanda had tried Jack next, but he'd been in the same predicament, saying Duke was impossible to shop for because he rarely wanted anything and when he did, he bought it.

With her hopes dwindling, she'd reached out to Jamie, Duke's sister. Jamie's suggestion had been a gift card to the local hardware shop, but that felt about as unromantic as could be to Amanda.

She wanted to get him something that held some meaning. Something that said she'd put thought and time into picking out the perfect thing for him.

So far, she was striking out. Big time. She went into the next shop, which was a men's clothing store. Duke was not a guy who dressed up, although he did once in a while. Like if they were going out to eat someplace.

Maybe she'd get him a really nice low-key Hawaiian shirt. Something silk and super luxurious. Something he might not otherwise buy for himself. It wasn't like he didn't have the money. He did, for sure, but he just didn't seem to splurge on things like that. Things for his boat, yes. But Amanda didn't know the first thing about what his boat might need and the last thing she wanted was to give him something he only had to return.

At this rate he was going to end up with nothing, though.

The one good thing in all of this was that thanks to Katie's generous help in getting them all invested in Owen's cryptocurrency venture, money was no longer an issue for Amanda. If she wanted to splurge on something for Duke, she could.

She let out a determined sigh and made herself concentrate. There was nothing wrong with a nice shirt. It said she appreciated the way he looked, and she valued their time together enough to give him something to show off his physique in. Didn't it? Or would he interpret it as her thinking he needed help getting dressed?

Why was this so hard? She loved the guy, for crying out loud. She just wanted the gift to reflect that.

But it was so much harder than it looked.

She walked through the shop once to get a feel for what they had.

"Can I help you?"

She smiled at the man behind the counter. "I'm trying to find a gift for my boyfriend but he's really hard to buy for."

The man nodded. "Doesn't have a lot of needs or needs nothing because he's already bought it?"

"Pretty much both of those." She laughed. It was good to be understood.

"What are his hobbies?"

"He's a woodworker—actually, he can build just about anything. He's crafty like that. He has a boat. Likes to fish. Spends time with me and his family. He reads. But his mom already bought him a book." She moaned softly. "None of that is helping, is it?"

The man held up a finger. "Maybe. How about a fishing shirt?"

"There are shirts for fishing?"

"Oh, yes. Marvelous product." He came out from around the counter. "Let me show you."

He directed her to a rack of long-sleeved, almost tissue-weight shirts with all sorts of vents in them designed to keep the wearer cool while also protected from the sun. She was sure she'd seen Duke in one of these now that she understood what it was, but it still seemed like a good gift.

He did love to fish. Just a few weeks ago he'd made dinner for her with a fish he'd caught. This was a gift that said some of what she wanted to say. And there was a nice pale blue that would complement his eyes.

She nodded. "I'll get one of these."

"What size do you think?"

She picked up a large, then an extra large to compare the two. Duke was tall and well-built with broad shoulders. Then she realized she didn't need to guess. "You know what? I think I'll text his mom and ask her to be sure."

In a last-minute decision, she texted Dixie *and* Jamie, just to make sure she'd reach one of them. *What size shirt would Duke wear?*

Jamie answered first. *Large.*

Dixie chimed in a couple seconds later. *Yes, large.*

Great, thank you! She put her phone away and smiled at the salesman. "I'll take the large."

"Wonderful. I'll ring it up for you."

With that purchase taken care of, she headed out to see what else she could find. The shirt was nice, but it wasn't enough. Duke was an incredibly special man who deserved more.

The three remaining shops in the little strip mall

were an ice cream shop, a children's store, and at the end, a large junk and antiques mart.

The ice cream shop was tempting but she didn't have time to treat herself. The children's shop was pointless. The junk and antique mart didn't give her much hope, but she was about out of time and opportunity.

She went in.

The large store's interior was divided into little booths, each one with its own items displayed. She could only imagine what Militant Marge would think of shopping here for Christmas presents. She'd be mortified, not only that Amanda might consider buying something used but also that she'd think such a thing was acceptable to give as a gift.

The idea sort of spurred Amanda on. Knowing Duke's family and their easygoing ways, they'd all probably think a secondhand gift was a great idea.

She knew her time was short, so she browsed with a sharp eye, but nothing jumped out at her. Most of it looked more suited to the junk description than the antique part. And she sincerely doubted Duke would be interested in a commemorative Charles and Diana wedding plate or a ceramic seagull.

"Hello there, young lady."

She turned to see a little old man in plaid trousers and a white button-down shirt sitting in the booth behind her. He wore a newsboy cap and thick glasses that magnified his twinkling eyes.

"Hi."

He pointed a gnarled finger at the bag from the men's clothing store. "Doing some shopping I see."

"I am. Trying to find a great gift for a great guy."

"Your husband?"

"Boyfriend." She looked around his booth. Not much of what he sold made sense to her. "Were all of these things yours?"

"Name's Jimmy. Some of them. But mostly I've collected them to sell so that they end up with people who want them instead of being discarded."

She nodded. "That's very nice, Jimmy. I'm Amanda, by the way."

"Pleasure to meet you, miss." He laughed. "You don't know what any of this is, do you, Amanda?"

She grinned. "No, I don't. What are they?"

He slapped his knee, clearly tickled by the exchange. He stood and hitched up his pants. He was a head shorter than her. "They don't make things like this anymore. These are the tools that were once valued in this country. The tools that built things, that made it possible for a man to make his life better. His family's life better. These are antique woodworking tools."

"Is that right?" Amanda drew in a soft breath, her smile widening. If there were ever things that Duke would appreciate, she was pretty sure she was looking at them.

"You betcha. I've got awls, scribes, planes, hand drills, vises, files, rasps, vintage screwdrivers and hammers, even some old spirit levels and a few draw knives. You could build a house with these. Or a table. Anything you need."

"What I need," Amanda said, "is a nice assortment of these." She gave him her full attention. "Jimmy, will you pick out three of the nicest ones? Three you think a woodworking man would like and appreciate the most?"

He rubbed his hands together. "You betcha."

Chapter Seventeen

Katie didn't feel like a grandmother but holding her new grandchild was unlike anything she'd ever experienced in her life. She already loved this baby with her entire being. She stared down at Gunner Alford, amazed by the sheer perfection of him. "He's just beautiful. Aren't you," she cooed. "And quite the chunk, too."

Josh laughed. "He was almost nine pounds at birth. Now at eight months, he's almost twenty-one pounds."

Christy, Josh's wife, smiled. "He's definitely an over-achiever."

Sophie opened the door and Dakota, Josh's four-year-old daughter, came running in. "Mom. Mom. *Mom*. We saw dophins."

Gage came in behind them.

Sophie laughed. "I love that she doesn't say the L."

Christy crouched down. "Did you see dolphins?"

Dakota held up her fingers. "Free of them."

Josh grinned, then looked at Owen. "I can't thank you enough for flying us down here and letting us stay at your place."

"You're very welcome," Owen said. "Most of the time it's pretty quiet around here. Nice to have company for a change. Especially this time of year."

Christy took a few steps toward Katie. "I hate to break up the party, but these two need to be in bed. And since Gunner is already asleep, I feel like I should take advantage of that."

Katie handed the baby over carefully, so she didn't wake him.

"Thanks," Christy said softly.

Josh took Dakota's hand. "I'd better help. Come on, kiddo. Let's go have story time then bed."

He glanced back at them. "Twenty minutes?"

Katie nodded. "Sounds good."

As he closed the door behind him, Katie let out a sigh. "Can you believe those are my *grandchildren?*"

Owen came to stand beside her. "You're pretty hot for a granny."

"It's Mimi, not Granny." Smiling, she cut her eyes at him. "But I'm going to let that go this one time, since you bought me a boat and all."

He laughed and put his arm around her. "It's really nice to have them all here. Although I can also see that it might be a little overwhelming."

"It's a lot to absorb. I realize I've known Josh for

almost a year now but knowing him and being in the same room as my son is still a bit surreal. In the best possible way."

Sophie was grinning. "Dakota might be my most favorite person in the world. She said I looked like a princess."

Gage's mouth twitched. "She's not wrong."

Katie giggled. It was so cute to see Owen's former-military security guy all moony-eyed over her sister. They made a great couple.

Rika, Owen's cook, came in. "Ready for eggnog and Christmas cookies?"

"In about ten minutes," Owen said.

She nodded. "I'll be back."

It was more like half an hour by the time Josh and Christy returned. She had a baby monitor in her hand. "I hope no one minds."

"Of course not," Katie said.

Rika came back as if summoned by magic and started setting out the cookies, before adding a pitcher of eggnog along with a bottle each of bourbon and dark rum. She put more things on the table: small plates, glasses, and napkins, then disappeared again.

Everyone helped themselves. Katie didn't add anything to her eggnog and she noticed that Christy didn't, either. The boys added bourbon, while Sophie put the tiniest splash of dark rum in hers.

They all took seats in the living room.

"So," Katie said. "What would you guys like to do tomorrow? Any thoughts?"

Josh shrugged and looked at Christy, who shrugged right back. He turned to Katie. "I think we're open for anything."

Christy nodded. "I'm sure Dakota would love to swim, but is the water warm enough for that?"

Owen swallowed the sip of eggnog he'd just taken. "The pool can be heated to whatever temperature you think she'd like. As for the gulf, it's like bathwater. If she wants to swim in that, we can head out on the boat to one of the sandbars where there's plenty of shallow water. And possibly see some more dolphins."

"That sounds great," Christy said. "I think I'd prefer her to swim in the pool, but that's probably just the overprotective mom in me talking."

Katie smiled. "Whatever you want is fine. I can show you around the resort, show you where I live. I know Iris would love to meet you. Or you can hang out by the pool and do nothing. We're really good at that around here."

Josh laughed. "This *is* sort of a vacation for us. Doing nothing holds a certain amount of appeal."

Christy's brows bent. "I'd feel bad not doing anything. We should at least get Dakota out on the boat. It would be a nice experience for her. She loved the short ride we took getting here."

Sophie leaned in. "She was so excited about those dolphins."

"Oh," Katie said. "I know what she might like. The resort just got a glass-bottom boat. I bet she'd enjoy that."

"That does sound fun," Christy said. "And safe." She laughed at herself. "I can't help it. I grew up in the Midwest and we went to a lake in the summers, so the ocean still seems like this enormous, slightly scary thing to me. I'm sure I'll get over it."

"It's okay," Katie reassured her. She got her phone out. "We'll do whatever you guys are comfortable with. Let me just text Eddie and see if there's a time that works for him to take us out."

"If not," Owen said. "Gage and I could probably drive it. If that would be okay."

She kept her eyes on the screen as she typed. "Let me see what he says."

Any availability for a glass-bottom boat tour tomorrow?

Eddie answered pretty quickly. *For your family? How many?*

She looked up. "He wants to know how many. Who's going?"

Owen held a hand up. "You take your family. Gage and I don't need to go if there aren't seats."

At least four adults plus one kid, one baby.

I can do that, Eddie texted back. *I only have four booked and the boat holds fourteen.*

Thank you! In that case, there will be six adults. Time?

10 a.m.

We'll see you there! Katie smiled at those around her. "We're all set for tomorrow at ten."

"All of us?" Owen asked.

She nodded. "Yep. The whole crew." She was really looking forward to it. An outing with her family. In every sense of the word.

Chapter Eighteen

Olivia's day started as it usually did, with coffee on the front porch. Although she'd be alone today. Eddie had left around four a.m. to take a couple of guests out fishing. But she'd seen him last night, so it wasn't too much of a hardship.

The crisp air felt nice. She tugged her cardigan around her a little tighter and held her mug in both hands, savoring the warmth coming through the ceramic. These cooler temperatures wouldn't last, so she needed to enjoy them while she could.

She went through the day's tasks in her head. Honestly, there weren't that many, since she'd accomplished so much in the last week. She'd done that purposefully to give herself time to get ready for the holiday, but even that was pretty well taken care of.

Maybe she'd stop by the spa. She'd promised Manuela and Leigh Ann both that she'd look over their pricing and profit margins to see if things could be tightened up anywhere. And she'd been wanting to learn the spa's new inventory software. All she needed was to sit down and give herself some time with it. She prided herself on being able to figure out things like that.

She picked up her phone and sent Leigh Ann a quick text. *Would you mind if I spent some time at the spa today going over those profit margins? I'm finally available.*

Leigh Ann answered back. *Help yourself. Use my office and my computer. Password is on a sticky note under the keyboard.*

Which was a terrible place for it, Olivia thought. But Leigh Ann probably already knew that. *Thanks. I'll let you know what I find.*

Looking forward to your report.

Olivia set the phone down and picked up her coffee again. She needed to drink faster. It was cooling off.

Just then her phone buzzed with a message. She checked the screen, expecting to see Leigh Ann again, but it was Jenny.

Are you around? Could I come by?

Of course! On the front porch.

On my way.

Since Jenny had moved in with Nick, Olivia didn't see her daughter quite as much. Jenny worked from home, after all, and was kept pretty busy these days, since the resort had brought her on part-time to handle some of their PR. But Olivia and Eddie had twice been to Nick's for dinner with them, and Nick and Jenny had been to dinner once at Eddie's and once at Olivia's.

It seemed to Olivia to be a very healthy, adult relationship. Something she still couldn't believe she had with her daughter.

Jenny showed up a few minutes later in leggings, a big sweatshirt that came to her thighs, and a knit cap.

Olivia almost laughed at the cap. "It's not that cold."

"Mom, it is definitely cold. After all those months of heat and sun? Yeah, I'm chilly."

"You want to go in?"

"No. I'm fine to sit on the porch. But I might go get a cup of that coffee. If you have more."

"There is. Help yourself."

Jenny went in, coming back out with a mug in her hands. She sat in the other chair.

"What's up?" Olivia asked.

"I don't even know where to start." She sighed. "Not true. I do. By just putting it out there. Nick's mom is arriving today. And she's staying with us."

Olivia blinked, not quite sure what to say. "Yolanda?"

Jenny nodded and sipped her coffee, little wisps of steam rising up. "The one and only."

"When did this all come about?"

"Like, just yesterday. I think. She apparently threatened to make waves if Nick didn't let her come. Oh, and this all started because she said he was being brainwashed by Iris and everyone here."

Olivia made a face. "Brainwashed. Please."

"You've heard about her from Iris. You know how she is."

"That is true." Olivia sighed. "She arrives today?"

"Yep. Around two, I think."

"Not much time to prepare." Olivia suddenly looked at her daughter. "Is that why you're here? Do you want to stay here while she's visiting?"

"No. I thought about it, trust me, but what kind of a girlfriend would I be if I abandoned Nick in his hour of need? I'm sure it's not going to be fun, but I'm staying. If there was ever a time to be at his side, this is it."

"I commend you. But my door is always open if you need to escape."

"Thanks. You never know." Jenny slouched in the chair a bit. "I am not looking forward to her being here. I'm sure that's the wrong attitude, but it's how I feel."

"I'm not sure it's the wrong attitude." Olivia glanced over at her daughter. "Aren't you afraid she'll make a target out of you?"

"Yes. Nick's afraid of that, too. But it doesn't show much backbone to run."

"I agree with you there. What's your game plan?"

"Be sweet and cordial without being a pushover. I do have the home-court advantage."

Olivia nodded. "You mind if I share this news with the girls?"

"That's one of the reasons I'm here. So you could rally the troops. We all need to be prepared for her."

Olivia didn't know how one prepared for a woman like Yolanda Oscott. "I assume Iris knows about this visit?"

"According to Nick, it was Iris's blessing that made him say yes."

Olivia narrowed her eyes. "Really?"

Jenny nodded. "Iris told him it was Christmas, so she was feeling generous."

That sounded like Iris. She was so excited for Christmas this year, which Olivia was thrilled about, but this was one gift she could have done without. "She probably knows that bad press right before we're about to open the new area of the resort wouldn't be great either."

"I'm sure she does. But look, if that happens, if Yolanda still tries to play dirty, I'll be all over it. I will use every trick in the book to quash whatever nonsense she puts out."

"I appreciate that." Olivia glanced at the time.

"You need to get moving?" Jenny asked.

"I do. But if you want to talk more, I can stop by after work."

Jenny shot her a look. "So you can meet Yolanda?"

"Oh. Right. She'll be there."

Jenny smiled, a gleam in her eyes. "You know, that's not a bad idea, actually. You stopping by, I mean. You did singlehandedly figure out the resort's funds were being embezzled and got almost nine million dollars of that money returned. There's no way Yolanda could find fault with that."

Olivia felt a sudden surge of panic. "So you really want me to come by?"

"Yes. We might need the break."

"Okay." There was no way she would say no to her daughter needing her. "I'll be there. Around four okay?"

"That would be great. We can sit and talk on the porch if it's nice."

Olivia just nodded. For Jenny, she could manage this. She didn't love confrontation, though. It made her nervous. Even if she was getting better about it. Being in her new position had given her some confidence. Even so, she hoped Yolanda behaved. Although maybe that was a miracle even Christmas couldn't pull off.

Chapter Nineteen

Iris had a small, sour pit in her stomach. Like fruit gone bad. But there was no turning back now. If she walked away from the dock, Yolanda would see her leaving and wouldn't *that* go over well.

Instead, Iris stood proudly beside Nick and Jenny and pretended she was happy to welcome Arthur's first wife to their home.

What else could she do? It had been her big idea to allow Yolanda to visit. She blamed the intoxicating influence of Christmas cheer. And a momentary lapse of reason.

Rico docked the pontoon, got the boat tied up, then offered Yolanda a hand to exit.

Iris had seen old photos of Yolanda. Very old. Which was what Yolanda was now. Not as old as Iris, granted, but the woman looked like she was in her early sixties but trying to pass as half that.

She wore white skinny jeans with white shearling boots and a sparkly red sweater that only seemed capable of covering one shoulder at a time. Her hair was a blond hurricane of teasing and spraying, accented with two rhinestone poinsettia clips.

Her false eyelashes reminded Iris of pillow fringe. She looked like a cocktail waitress at a casino at the North Pole.

Iris did her best to smile pleasantly, even though she secretly wanted to scrape a fingernail down Yolanda's face just to see how many layers of makeup she actually had on. "Welcome to Compass Key, Yolanda."

Yolanda stepped off the boat. Rico hauled her bags to the dock. Three of them.

Iris wondered just how long Yolanda planned on staying.

She lifted her chin and took a long look around. "To think, this could have all been mine." She looked at Nick. "And should have been yours."

"*Mom*." He shook his head. "We've been through all of that. Please don't start or I will put you right back on that boat for the mainland."

Yolanda lifted her hands, her fingers covered in bejeweled rings, wrists dripping in bracelets, nails long and holly berry red. "That's all I wanted to say."

Iris doubted it. She kept smiling anyway. Years of working in the hospitality industry had taught her that a smile didn't have to be connected to the heart to be believed. "Well, I'm sure you want to get settled in. I thought I could give you a little tour of the place on the way back to the house, if you like."

"Actually," Yolanda said. "I'm famished. The meal in First Class was fish and I don't eat fish."

Nick heaved out a breath. "Mom, you're in the middle of one of the biggest fresh seafood areas in the country. You're really not going to eat fish?"

"Not on a plane," Yolanda said. "If what's offered here is actually fresh, then yes, I will try it."

"Oh, it's definitely fresh," Jenny said. "And it's absolutely delicious."

Yolanda suddenly seemed to notice there was a young woman standing next to her son. "And you are?"

Nick's face spoke volumes. "Mom, this is Jenny. I told you all about her."

"Oh, yes, right. You tweet for a living."

"It's quite a lot more than just tweeting," Jenny said.

Iris wondered if Jenny's smile was much like her own. Mostly for show.

"Perhaps you can tell me about it at lunch," Yolanda said. "Although I would like to catch up with my son. He's the reason I'm here. I'm sure you can understand."

"Absolutely," Jenny said.

"So." Yolanda looked around. "Is there somewhere to eat around here?"

"Yes," Nick answered. "My house. The dining facilities are for paying guests." He smiled. "But you're my guest, so I'm happy to feed you."

This, Iris thought, was her moment to be the gracious host. "Why don't we visit The Palms? I'll take care of lunch."

Nick looked at her, obviously surprised but trying to hide it. "That's very generous of you, Iris."

Her smile came easier this time. "It's my pleasure." She stepped to the side. "Rico, will you call a porter and have Ms. Oscott's bags taken to the house?"

"Yes, ma'am, Miss Iris."

"Thank you." Iris looked at Nick and his mother again. "Shall we?"

The Palms was quiet, as Iris imagined it would be at this hour. Too late for lunch, far too early for dinner, but that was ideal. Very few people would have to listen to Yolanda's observations. Such as they were.

They were ushered to a table in the corner and given menus. Water glasses were delivered promptly, and their server greeted them with enthusiasm. "What an honor it is to have you with us today, Miss Iris."

"I'm happy to be here."

"May I tell you about the specials?"

"Please," Iris said.

"We have a grilled grouper on sourdough toast with housemade tartar sauce, lettuce, tomato, and sweet pickled red onions. That comes with your choice of French fries, sweet potato fries, coleslaw, side salad, or fruit. We also have teriyaki pork skewers with red and green peppers, onion, and pineapple. That's served on a bed of coconut rice. Our dessert today is a coconut flan, and we also have a mango rum sorbet."

"Those sound great," Jenny said.

Yolanda looked unimpressed. "I'm going to need a minute."

So much for being famished.

The server nodded. "I'll be back in a bit to check on you."

Iris already knew what she was having. The protein salad. David had created it especially for her, since she'd changed her diet, and even though it wasn't on the menu, he'd made sure it would always be available and that all the cooks knew how to create it.

The protein salad wasn't that complicated. Steak, chicken, or seafood on a bed of baby greens, along with a quartered hard-boiled egg, halved heirloom cherry tomatoes, blue cheese crumbles, real bacon bits, and roasted pepitas, which added the nicest crunch.

He paired it with a creamy buttermilk avocado dressing that he'd come up with as well. He really was a treasure.

Jenny put her menu down. "That grouper sandwich sounds great to me."

"Me, too," Nick said.

The server returned. "Are you ready for me to take your orders?"

Iris didn't wait for Yolanda to answer. "I'll have the protein salad with grouper."

"Excellent." The server nodded and looked at Yolanda. "And for you, ma'am?"

Yolanda still had her menu open. "I don't see a protein salad."

"It's not on the menu. It's a dish created especially for Miss Iris by Chef David. It's a high-protein, low-carb option that we always have available."

Yolanda sniffed. "Must be nice. But I suppose things like that are pretty standard when you own your own island."

Iris leaned in. "Anyone can order that salad, Yolanda. It's just not on the menu yet because we saw no reason to reprint the menu for one item. It'll be added when the spring menus are printed. If you want it, get it."

Yolanda pursed her lips and closed her menu. "I'll just have the pork kabobs."

Iris barely resisted the urge to roll her eyes. Arthur had repeatedly told her that his ex-wife had three hobbies: Gold-digging, herself, and being a martyr.

Iris had always shaken her head and told him he must be exaggerating just a little. Someday, when she was reunited with him, she'd have to apologize for doubting him.

Chapter Twenty

Grace stepped in to help at The Palms for the dinner shift when the floor manager's car wouldn't start and he couldn't make it in. Working a shift was no big deal. She'd had a fairly light day with only interviews in the morning, then she'd put a few hours in at Castaways, showing the workers where the cold cases were supposed to go.

Filling in for the floor manager was actually pretty fun. Besides keeping an eye on things, it meant she got to do table visits to check in with the diners to see how they were enjoying their meals. She liked talking to guests and hearing how much they enjoyed the food, then getting to tell them that the chef was her husband.

It was a great chance to let them know about the cookbook available in the resort's boutique, too.

She also backed up the servers wherever they needed it. She filled water glasses, brought odds and

ends to the tables that needed things, even helped run
food. Now and then she'd send a table a free dessert or
see to it that a special occasion was properly cele-
brated. Sometimes, she'd just answer questions for the
guests, or suggest fun things to do in the area. Whatever they were interested in.

In general, working as floor manager was one of
her favorite ways to spend an evening in any restaurant. Before her drinking had become a problem, it was
how she'd spent most of her evenings at the restaurant
she and David had owned. The front of the house had
always been her domain.

It felt good not only to have the drinking behind
her, but to be back in the saddle, as it were. She loved
interacting with guests, even though she still had to
take care of more managerial things, like calm down a
server who'd forgotten to put an order in, something
she was able to expedite by letting David know, or help
another server who'd taken the wrong meals to the
wrong tables.

Working like that made her realize that she
wouldn't mind doing the job again full-time, but of
course, Curt had been hired to take the position at
Castaways and Iris's when they opened. And her job
now was still front of house, but not in such a
hands-on way.

David wanted to bring Curt in as soon as possible
to get him up to speed on the resort and train him on

how they expected Iris's and Castaways to be run. It would be Curt and Grace's job to train all of the incoming front-of-house people. Servers, cashiers, hosts, food runners, bartenders, and even bussers, so it was important he got trained himself and was ready to go.

In fact, David was talking about starting with him the week after Christmas, although the staff bungalow that would be Curt's new living quarters wouldn't be ready until probably the first or second week of the new year. She'd have to check with Jack Shaw about that.

As she floated through the dining room, her gaze coasting over the tables and diners to look for any potential issues or places she could help, she thought about what it would be like to work and live so closely with Curt.

But her thoughts got shoved aside by Lala Queen sweeping into The Palms with several of her friends. Lala was in a white catsuit with a Chanel chain belt, furry pink boots, and a gold sequin duster.

She clearly hadn't come to Compass Key to hide away from attention or be treated like a normal person. At least that was Grace's impression. She'd gotten Leigh Ann's email about dealing with potentially diffi-cult guests, too, so Grace took a deep breath and walked over to greet the singer.

"Good evening. Table for four?"

Lala didn't answer, but the woman Grace understood to be Lala's personal assistant did. "Six, actually. There are two more of our party on the way."

"Great. Just give me a minute and I'll get that set up for you."

"Ms. Queen has to be seated where she can see the door, preferably with her back to the wall and not other people. She doesn't like anyone behind her."

"I'll do my best to make that accommodation." Special seating requests weren't that big of a deal. Grace went off to find a table that would work for six and give Lala the seat she wanted. She found the perfect spot, a round six-top in the corner, but it wasn't cleaned yet, as the last diners were only just getting up.

She got the attention of Mike, one of the bussers. "I need that six-top next."

He nodded. "You got it."

"Thank you." She went back up front, smiling at Lala's group. "We're getting the table ready now. It'll just be a few minutes."

"Thanks," the assistant said.

Grace nodded. "I'm Grace, by the way. I'm the MOD this evening, so if there's anything else I can do to help, please let me know."

"I'm Marta," the woman said. "And there might be, so thank you for the offer." She hesitated like she had more to say. Which, apparently, she did. "Lala only drinks *good* bottled water. Voss would be her preference."

"We can take care of that," Grace said. Lala's people had listed Voss as one of the group's special dietary requirements, which was silly, because how could a *brand* be a special dietary requirement, but Grace knew there was a case of it in the cooler reserved for Lala already. There was another case at the bar by the pool.

The resort did things like that for guests all the time. It was all part and parcel of catering to the sort of clientele that came here.

"And she's just gone vegan two days ago, so can you let the chef know that her food really needs to be vegan. Like, a hundred percent." Marta glanced toward Lala, who was taking a selfie. "She'll freak otherwise."

"Don't worry. Our kitchen is equipped to handle all sorts of dietary requirements." David wasn't a fan of vegan cooking. He loved butter and bacon and duck fat and all those sorts of delicious things, but he could cook anything and obviously would. Guest satisfaction was key. He even kept a separate grill in the kitchen just for preparing vegan meals so that there would be no chance of cross-contamination, such as it was.

Mike went by, giving Grace a nod. She picked up six menus. "If you'll follow me, your table is ready."

She got them seated, noticing a few heads turning as Lala walked through. Apparently, there were celebrities that even other celebrities found interesting. Although it would be hard not to look at a woman dressed like a Bratz doll.

As they got seated, Grace handed out the menus. "Your server will be right with you to tell you about tonight's specials. Enjoy your meal."

She went back to work, only to have that table's server, Josephine, find her several minutes later.

Josephine stood with her back to Lala's table and spoke quietly. "I need some help."

"What's going on?"

"Lala wants the grouper special, but vegan."

Grace narrowed her eyes as she recalled the explanation of that special. "The grouper special is filet of grouper topped with ginger crab butter, served with pork fried rice and seared baby bok choy that I'm pretty sure is cooked in lard."

Josephine nodded. "Yep. And I did explain that to her, but she insisted that the chef make it vegan for her."

Grace took a breath. "Let me talk to her."

She put on a bright smile and went over. "Hi there." She looked directly at Lala. "I understand you'd like to order one of our specials this evening but in a vegan version."

"That's right," Lala said.

"That's no problem. I just want to make sure you understand a vegan version of the grouper special will be plain rice and steamed bok choy, although we could certainly substitute the pork fried rice with coconut rice if you'd prefer."

Lala stared at her. "Coconut rice sounds good. But, like, make sure the grouper is cooked all the way through. I don't like raw fish."

Grace nearly bit her tongue. "That's not a problem, as there won't be any grouper. Fish isn't vegan."

The rest of Lala's party was curiously quiet or occupied with their phones. It didn't surprise her that none of them had explained it to their boss.

"But I want the fish. Just the vegan kind." Lala frowned. "Wait. Is it a whole fish? Because I can't eat anything with a face."

"No, the grouper portion is a six- to seven-ounce filet."

"That's what I want," she said. "But, like, the vegan version. No face on anything or I swear I will send it back."

That was what Grace wanted to avoid. Wasted food because of a misunderstanding. Not to mention a guest who was upset their meal wasn't right, all because they didn't know what they were asking for. "We can do that, so long as you understand the fish, regardless of how it's portioned or cooked, is still considered meat and therefore not vegan."

Lala looked confused. "Fish isn't vegan?"

Grace shook her head. As hard as it was to believe, she'd had similar conversations several times before in her career in the restaurant business. "No, but I believe fish with rice and vegetables could be considered pescatarian."

Lala twirled a couple of blond and pink braids around one finger. "I don't care about that. I'm totally not religious."

One of the men at the table snorted, but quickly covered it up with a cough.

Grace just nodded. "So the grouper, with no ginger crab butter, coconut rice, and steamed bok coy?"

Lala nodded. "Yeah, that."

Grace looked at Josephine. "I'll sort it with David."

Josephine mouthed a silent thank you and Grace went off to the kitchen, unable to keep from smiling. Wait until the girls heard about this one.

Leigh Ann would laugh herself silly.

Chapter Twenty-one

After hearing from Olivia about Yolanda Oscott's arrival, Leigh Ann couldn't help but join Olivia when she dropped in on Nick, Jenny, and their *guest*. Leigh Ann figured at the very least she could offer moral support to Nick, Jenny, and Olivia.

But mostly, she wanted to see the infamous Yolanda for herself.

"Nervous?" she asked Olivia as they walked up the steps to Nick's third-floor suite.

"A little," Olivia answered. "But more for Jenny than myself."

"I get that," Leigh Ann said. "It's natural to want to protect your child."

Olivia nodded. "That's exactly it. I want to protect her. I know she's an adult, but I still feel that way."

"They never stop being our babies, no matter how old they get, no matter how many of their own babies they have."

They reached the landing and Olivia knocked.

"Hey," Leigh Ann. "You're not even out of breath."

Olivia smiled. "It's all those laps I've been doing. Plus, all the walking around here."

The door opened and Jenny's eyes widened in happy surprise. "Mom! And Leigh Ann! How nice of you both to stop by." She whispered, "Perfect timing." Then in her normal voice said, "Come on in."

Nick and Yolanda weren't instantly visible, then Leigh Ann saw them through the windows on the opposite side of the house. The sliders were all open and Nick and his mother were sitting out on the porch.

"Can I get you guys something to drink? I've got white wine, coconut water, plain water, sparkling water…"

Olivia laughed. "Sparkling water sounds great." She lowered her voice. "How's it going?"

Jenny exhaled. "It's going. What can I get for you, Leigh Ann?"

"Is anyone else drinking?"

Jenny nodded. "Yolanda's having white wine."

"Same for me then."

"I'll bring the drinks out if you want to head to the porch."

"Thanks, honey," Olivia said.

Leigh Ann walked with her outside. Yolanda was on the couch against the wall and Nick was seated in the adjacent chair.

He stood as they arrived. "Afternoon. Thanks for coming by." He gestured at Olivia. "Yolanda, this is Jenny's mom, Olivia. And this is Leigh Ann, her friend, and the director of the fitness center and spa."

"Nice to meet you," Olivia said.

Yolanda looked them over with a thin smile.

Jenny came out with the drinks. Nick brought another chair over, which Leigh Ann took, letting Olivia have the other seat on the couch.

Leigh Ann sipped her wine, then spoke to Yolanda. "How was your trip here?"

"Fine," Yolanda said. She turned her attention to Olivia. "Nick told me you're an accountant?"

"That's right," Olivia answered. "I handle the books, payroll, some inventory. All of that."

Jenny, who'd taken the chair on the other end of the couch, nodded enthusiastically. "Thanks to my mom's skills, she was able to figure out that the former accountant was skimming and had been for years."

Leigh Ann chimed in. "She was getting help from her boyfriend, who was the head chef at the resort at that time."

Yolanda's brows moved slightly. "You might want to consider who you hire more carefully."

Leigh Ann watched Olivia's face.

Olivia's jaw seemed to set a certain way. "We didn't hire those individuals. And since their arrests, they've both been replaced. The accountant by me, obviously, and the new chef is married to Grace, another of the new owners. A man named David McKellen. His cookbook featuring dishes served here at the resort just came out."

Yolanda sipped her wine.

Olivia wasn't done, though. "I understand it's been some time since you've seen Nick. It must be nice to be reunited with him. Especially in a beautiful spot like this. Do you have anything planned for your stay?"

"It's always good to see my son," Yolanda said. "But I didn't come here for a vacation. I came to check on his wellbeing."

Olivia made a face. "His wellbeing?" She looked at Nick like this was news to her. "You're all right, aren't you?"

Nick laughed. "My mother is just being...a mom."

Olivia smiled and turned back to Yolanda. "I can understand that. Leigh Ann and I were just talking about how we always want to protect our children, no matter their ages. But you have so much to be proud of Nick for. After all, he saved Iris's life."

"Well," Nick said. "That makes it sound like I did more than anyone else would have done."

Leigh Ann decided to add her two cents. "You did figure out she had that B12 deficiency. If not for that and her amazing recovery, she'd probably be off in that home in Kentucky right now. Don't belittle what you did. It really was lifesaving."

Yolanda glared at her son. "You mean she was going to leave the island?"

"Yes," Olivia answered for him. "She was planning on moving away from her home and everything she and Arthur built. Wouldn't that have been sad?"

Yolanda just pursed her lips. To Leigh Ann, she didn't look like she thought that was sad at all.

Jenny stood up. "If you'll excuse me, I think I'll bring the hors d'oeuvres out." She went into the kitchen.

Yolanda watched her go before speaking again. "I understand your daughter's entire career centers around social media. That must have been a disappointment for you and your husband."

"I'm divorced," Olivia said. "And I've never been disappointed in my daughter's career choices a day in her life. She's her own woman and has never had a problem going after what she wants. She's very successful."

Yolanda snorted as a superior grin settled over her face. "I'm happy for you if you're satisfied with that, but I set a much higher bar for my son. Being a doctor is a sacrifice few are equipped to make."

Nick cut his eyes at his mother. "Mom—"

Leigh Ann cleared her throat. "Jenny's three biggest clients are Mother's Resort, best-selling author Iris Deveraux, and multibillionaire Owen Monk. I'd say she's set her own bar pretty high."

Yolanda's smug look faded a bit. "Owen Monk? I understand he has a house on the island."

"He does," Leigh Ann said. "He's engaged to another of our friends, Katie Walchech. She's the communications director. Anyway, Jenny is a junior partner in her public relations firm and they thought so highly of her performance that she's single-handedly been put in charge of the satellite office here. She's a real catch."

Nick grinned. "Yeah, she is."

Jenny came back out with a plate of cubed cheese, sliced meats, and crackers, and another of cut-up veggies with a dip that looked very much like the resort's famous green goddess dressing. She put the plates on the table, along with a little stack of cocktail napkins. "What did I miss?"

Olivia helped herself to a cube of cheese. "We were just talking about your job and your amazing clients."

Jenny sat. "It is pretty great to work for the people I do." She dipped a cucumber slice in the dressing. "And all while living here. Honestly, this is about the most beautiful place I've ever been. Some days I wake up wondering if it was all just a dream, then I see the palm trees and the blue sky and I feel blessed all over again."

Yolanda shrugged with practiced indifference. "There are a lot of beautiful places in the world."

Jenny looked at Nick, still smiling. "But I'm blessed for other reasons, too."

He smiled right back, and Leigh Ann felt the warmth of the love between them. It was so sweet and wonderful. She glanced at Olivia, who was smiling broadly.

Yolanda, however, was frowning.

Leigh Ann couldn't stop herself. Enough was enough. "Why do you look so miserable, Yolanda? Aren't you happy for your son?"

Yolanda whipped around to face her. "Would you be happy if you found out your son was living with a woman you didn't even know? That he'd given up his job to work at a...a *resort* like this?"

"If he was happy, then why shouldn't I be, too? After all, it's his life, not mine. He's allowed to make his own choices. He should be, if he's an adult." Leigh Ann looked at Nick. "Your son has spent nearly the entirety of his career helping the less fortunate, sacrificing his own personal comfort to give of his time and talents. Now, because of the generosity of his late father and the goodness of his stepmother's heart, his life has taken another direction. And he's found love. If I were his mother, I'd be overjoyed for him."

Yolanda set her wineglass on the table with such force that the wine nearly splashed out. She stood. "Well, you're not his mother, so it doesn't matter what you think."

Then she strode off, back into the house. A few seconds later, a door slammed.

Leigh Ann sighed. "I'm really sorry. That wasn't my intention, but she kind of got me riled up. I feel like a terrible guest." She got up. "I'll go apologize."

"No," Nick said. "You have nothing to apologize for. What you said was the truth. She isn't happy for me. She thinks something nefarious is going on here, although I can't imagine what she thinks that is. Plus, she thinks Jenny's after me for my money, which is pretty rich coming from her."

He shook his head. "I said she could come to visit and stay with me. I never promised I was going to indulge her nonsense." He looked at Jenny again. "What matters is our life going forward. That's my priority. If my mother can't be happy for us, well then..."

"I love you," Jenny whispered.

He gave her a little smile. "I love you, too."

"I love both of you," Olivia said. "Now, I think Leigh Ann and I should get out of your hair."

"I agree to both of those things." Leigh Ann still felt bad. But she knew from experience that some people's minds just couldn't be changed.

Especially when, like Yolanda, they were just determined to be right. Even if they weren't.

Chapter Twenty-two

*D*inner could wait. So could changing out of her work clothes. Amanda dug straight into wrapping Duke's gifts as soon as she got home. The fishing shirt was easy, because the nice man at the clothing shop had put it in a box for her already. She finished that one first and tucked it under the tree.

The tools she'd bought from Jimmy were going to be a little harder. If she wrapped them as they were, Duke would probably figure out what they were by the shapes alone. He was handy like that.

She needed boxes to put them in, but she didn't have any. Maybe some of the other girls did, but she doubted it. Most of them had moved here with as little as possible. Boxes in which to wrap gifts probably hadn't been on anyone's list of necessities.

She thought hard, looking around the bungalow for something that might work.

She went over to the pantry and opened it. Inspiration struck. She took a few things out and brought them to the counter. The oats went into a glass storage jar she'd been meaning to put them in anyway. Two boxes of crackers were emptied as well, the sleeves of crackers going into a large Ziploc baggie to keep them fresh.

She surveyed the gifts once again. With Jimmy's help, she'd ended up with an awl, a plane, an antique brass spirit level, and a set of screwdrivers with wooden handles. She hadn't been able to limit herself to three, even if she wasn't sure the tools were all that practical. But they had history and she thought that was something Duke would like.

Plus, they showed she got who he was as a person.

She wrapped the screwdrivers individually in tissue paper then slipped the whole set into one of the cracker boxes and taped it up. The plane fit diagonally into the other cracker box and the awl went into the cylinder that had held the oats.

There was no box that would hold the spirit level. It was long and heavy and would have probably made a decent weapon. She supposed she could wrap it just as it was and hope for the best.

She unrolled her gift paper and started covering the other containers first. As she did, she finished that roll and was left with the cardboard tube. She tried slipping the spirit level into it, just to see if it would fit. It did.

Problem solved.

That tube was all she had left to wrap when a knock sounded at her door. That someone tried the knob, but she'd locked the door on purpose. It was probably Duke. "Just a sec," she called out.

She ran to the door and opened it a crack so he couldn't really see in.

Duke smiled at her. "Hey there. Did you just get home? You're still in your work shirt."

"I've been home a little bit. Just got occupied with a few things." She inhaled his scent. He looked and smelled freshly showered. He must have come over right after. "What are you up to?"

"I was going to broil some shrimp and scallops I picked up at the market the other day. You want to join me? If you haven't eaten dinner yet." His eyes narrowed. "Why are you holding the door like that?"

"I haven't eaten yet and the door is like this because Christmas things are happening inside."

"And I'm not allowed to see that?"

"Nope." She grinned. "Is ten minutes okay? I can bring a salad."

"Sure." He tipped his head like he was trying to see past her.

"Oh, no, you don't." She closed the door. "Ten minutes!"

She could hear him laughing. "Okay. Bring butter, too. I forgot to get some at the store."

"All right." She locked the door, just because he was sneaky, then went back to her wrapping.

She finished up the spirit level and put all of the gifts under her tree. Once again, she wondered if her tree didn't look a little bare with its simple white lights and gold and cream ornaments. It was still pretty and with Christmas about to be here, she wasn't going to run out and buy more ornaments for it.

Next year, though. Maybe she'd add another color. Turquoise to go with the tropical theme that everything seemed to have around here? Militant Marge would never approve of turquoise on a Christmas tree.

Amanda smiled at that thought, but the smile faded fast. The truth was, she missed her mother. Not her judgment or her rules or her attitude about most things in life, but there was definitely an empty place inside Amanda where her mother should have been.

Rekindling her relationship with Denise had been a very good thing. So had fixing her relationship with her children. Both of those had helped a lot.

But you only had one mother.

And Amanda's didn't want anything to do with her. All because of the choices Amanda had made to move to Compass Key and, as her mother would say, take up with Duke.

Was she really supposed to deny her own happiness for a woman who'd probably never been happy a day in her life?

That was too high of a price to pay.

Trying to shake the melancholy that thought left her with, Amanda went back to the kitchen and made the salad she'd promised to bring to Duke's. Lettuce with cucumbers, tomatoes, sliced mushrooms, a little sweet onion, some red pepper left over from the night before, and a sprinkling of toasted walnut pieces she'd been meaning to use up.

She covered the bowl with cling wrap, then ran upstairs to change. She went with jeans and a soft, cozy sweater.

She came back down, stuck her key in one pocket and her phone in another, then picked up the salad, took a stick of butter out of the fridge, and headed next door to Duke's.

She knocked.

"It's open," he called out.

She went in. He was in the kitchen, prepping.

"Hi."

"Hi." He smiled, then his brows went up. "Only one stick of butter?"

"You need more?"

He glanced at the pan on the stove. "No, I can make that work."

She put the salad on the raised bar counter, then brought the butter to him. "I can run back and get another one."

"No, it's all good." He put an arm around her and

kissed her. "Besides, I've had a long day of not being with you. I'd rather have you here with me than have more butter."

She leaned into him. "Hard day?"

He shrugged. "We're at that stage in the construction where one hiccup could really set us back. Trying to keep an eye on it all while troubleshooting all the little details just makes for a long day."

"Well, let me help. What can I do?"

"Do you know how to make cocktail sauce?"

"Sure, I can do that." She opened his fridge and looked around, taking out ketchup, lemon juice, Worcestershire sauce, and horseradish. Duke had a surprisingly well-stocked refrigerator and pantry for a single guy, but he enjoyed cooking.

She got a bowl and started adding the ingredients.

"Hot sauce, too," Duke said. "Couple drops anyway."

"Okay."

He was melting butter in the pan. The scallops sat on a plate nearby, waiting to be seared. "You're awfully quiet."

"Am I? Sorry. Just thinking, I guess."

"About your mom?"

She glanced at him. "How did you know that?"

He used tongs to pick the fat scallops up and place them one by one into the hot pan. They sizzled and spit. "It's Christmastime. Family is on a lot of people's minds. Seemed logical."

She stirred the cocktail sauce ingredients together. "It's like the one missing piece of the puzzle that is my life, you know?"

He nodded. "I can imagine. I'm sorry things haven't changed between you two. If you want to talk, you know I'm here."

"I do. And I appreciate that. It will help a lot to be with your family for Christmas."

"I'm glad. I know they love you."

Amanda smiled. "And I love them."

She truly did. But seeing Duke with his family, their easy interactions, their great affection for one another, the obvious love they all shared, just made the gulf between her and her mother seem that much wider.

Chapter Twenty-three

Katie loved watching Dakota in the pool. Owen had ordered and paid for overnight shipping on a big inflatable dolphin raft. Dakota was playing with it now. Ordering it around, actually, like it was a real dolphin under her command.

Katie laughed. "Kids are amazing."

Christy, seated next to her, nodded. "After that glass-bottom boat tour today, I think she's going to be a sea baby for a long time to come."

"That was pretty amazing," Katie agreed.

"I had no idea there was so much wildlife around here." Christy looked at her. "Thank you so much for setting that up for us. I've never seen a real live sea turtle. Or a stingray. Or any of those things. But the dolphins were kind of life-changing. If she knew what a marine biologist was, I'm pretty sure she'd want to be one."

Josh, on the other side of Christy, laughed. "You're

right about that." He was leaning forward on the lounge chair, one foot on either side of it. "Today was really cool." He looked down at Owen on the other side of Katie. "Thank you again for letting us stay here."

"Anytime," Owen said. "I mean that. I'm not always here but that doesn't mean you can't use one of the guest cottages. Katie's about to be my wife. That means what's mine is hers."

Josh laughed. "I can't believe Owen Monk is about to be my stepdad."

Owen laughed. "I've always wanted to send someone to their room."

That got them all chuckling.

Owen sat up a little straighter. "You know, we should all go out to my ranch in Montana next summer. It's incredible out there that time of year."

Katie smiled. "I would love to see your ranch. If I can get the time off, I'd love to go."

"You really mean that?" Josh asked.

"Absolutely." Owen nodded.

"Wow, that would be great," Josh said. "Summers are really the only time off I get, other than Christmas break and some time at Easter. Being a teacher means I'm on the same schedule the kids are."

Christy nodded. "Which works out pretty good. Or will, when Dakota starts kindergarten."

Gage and Sophie came out of the house, walking

hand in hand. Seeing that still made Katie smile. They let go of each other as they got closer.

Gage pushed his sunglasses up onto his head. "Rika says dinner will be ready in about twenty minutes."

Owen nodded, then looked around at the rest of them. "Should we just eat out here? It's certainly a beautiful night for dining al fresco. And I can always turn the lights on."

Katie knew they were eating earlier than usual to accommodate the kids' schedules, but she didn't mind. "I love the idea of eating out here."

"Yeah," Josh said. "So do I. It's not something we'd ever get to do this time of year back home."

Christy laughed. "That's for sure. And I have no doubt Dakota would eat in the pool on that raft if she could."

Gage smiled. "I'll let Rika know."

He went back toward the house, but Sophie took a seat next to Josh, her gaze going straight to Dakota. She waved at the little girl. "I love that child. She makes me want one."

Josh shrugged. "You're still young enough. Right?"

Sophie grinned. "You're my favorite nephew, you know that?" She shook her head. "I'm forty-three. I think that's pushing it."

Katie leaned forward. "You could always adopt."

Sophie looked at Josh again before answering. "I

could. But I'm not exactly headed toward the altar anytime soon and I think it's harder for single women."

She shook her head. "It's just being around Dakota and Gunner. They're giving me baby fever."

Owen leaned toward Katie. "You, too?"

"Maybe if I were younger. I don't know. Sometimes I wish I hadn't been so married to my career. That I'd gotten married and had kids and done all of that." She smiled at him. "But then I might not have met you."

He smiled.

She winked at him. "I'm really good with the path my life has taken."

"I'm glad things worked out the way they did, too."

She leaned in to kiss his cheek.

Gage came back out with a tray of plates, silverware, napkins, and tall plastic glasses.

Christy jumped up. "I can set the table." She wiggled her fingers at Josh. "You keep an eye on the kids."

"Always," he said.

Sophie got up, too. "I'll help."

Josh checked on Gunner, who was asleep in his carrier, then looked at Katie. "Will you keep an eye on him so I can go hang out with Dakota?"

"Happy to," she answered. He got up and walked toward the edge of the pool closest to where Dakota was playing.

"This is so nice," Katie said softly and to no one in

particular. Then she reached over and took Owen's hand. "I think this might be my most favorite Christmas ever. Even without the boat."

He laughed. "So I could have gotten you a kayak and you'd have been just as happy?"

She chuckled. "Actually, yes. But you can't take the pontoon back now."

"I wouldn't dream of it. Maybe we should all go out on it tomorrow? A little Christmas Eve cruise."

"That sounds nice. I don't think I'm ready to drive, though. I'd be happy to leave that up to you or Gage. Not saying I wouldn't be willing to take a turn behind the wheel, just that I don't want to be the captain."

"Not a problem."

She could have stared at him a lot longer, but she didn't want him to think she was acting weird.

The truth was, his questions had given her questions. Did Owen ever think about having kids? Did he regret not having them?

At nearly fifty, that ship had sailed for her. Didn't mean adoption wasn't still possible, but that was like beginning a brand-new life. They both had careers that kept them very busy. He travelled a lot, too, which would mean the heavy-lifting of parenting would often fall on her.

Sure, they could afford to hire help, but that didn't sit right with her. Not the kind of help that was basically substitute parenting, anyway.

If she was going to have a child, she wanted to be the one raising it.

She hoped he wasn't feeling like he was missing out on a part of life. Not when that part seemed like something she really couldn't give him.

Chapter Twenty-four

Olivia sat on her front porch staring out at the water and the darkening sky. The temperature was dropping, and the breeze was picking up, making it even cooler than the night before. Still really good weather for someone who'd spent the last part of her life in Ohio dealing with winters that seemed to never end.

She'd take sixty degrees in December any day.

She checked the time. Eddie would be getting home soon. That was half the reason she was sitting out here. Just to see him.

Hopefully, he'd have some ideas about a potential new hire for the marina. She really didn't want him to keep working such long hours. He wasn't as young as Rico and even though Eddie was fit, she didn't want him to get burned out, either.

She smiled at the Christmas lights wrapped

around her porch railing. They were so cheery. Just like the wreath on her door and her little tree.

Those decorations and the ones all over the resort really helped it feel like Christmas, because without the truly cold weather and snow, it wasn't quite the same.

Didn't mean she didn't still love it here. She was hooked on this place. Which only made her question Yolanda's sour attitude even more.

How could anyone be so miserable in a place like this? Did Yolanda really think Jenny was such a bad match for her son?

Olivia knew she was biased, but she wasn't so biased that she couldn't accurately take her own daughter's measure.

Jenny *was* a catch. Smart, pretty, talented, well-employed, and she obviously adored Nick. Who seemed to adore her right back.

Yolanda just didn't like the idea that she was losing her son to the place that represented her ex-husband's true happiness.

That had to be it.

Yolanda hated Compass Key because it was the place Arthur had found his purpose. And he'd spent the rest of his life here with Iris, the woman who was everything Yolanda wasn't.

Olivia imagined that had to be a pretty bitter pill to

swallow. But why couldn't Yolanda move on and find her own happiness?

Wasn't that what life was about?

She was thinking about going inside for a cup of decaf when she heard whistling. She smiled. Eddie.

She went down the steps to greet him. "Howdy, neighbor."

He smiled as soon as he saw her. "*Hola, mamacita.* How was your day?"

She lifted her brows. "Interesting. How was yours?"

"Long and not interesting. Let me get a shower and something to eat and I'll come over so you can tell me all about your day."

"If you're okay with meatloaf and a side of green beans, I can fix you a plate and you can eat here."

"You're too good to me. I'll be over in fifteen minutes."

"Take your time." She put her hands on his chest and kissed him. "You're worth waiting for."

His smile got a little bigger, his teeth bright white against his darkly tanned skin. "Maybe ten minutes now."

She laughed. "Hurry up then."

He went off to his place and she went inside to fix him that plate. She'd actually bought a small container of mashed potatoes, premade, thinking that she'd make him a plate and take it to him at some point, but this worked out.

She'd made the meatloaf and eaten when she'd gotten back from Nick's, but she'd happily sit with Eddie while he had his dinner.

It really was closer to fifteen minutes when he returned, knocking right before he opened the door. She was just putting his plate on the breakfast bar. "What do you want to drink?"

He held up two root beers. "After today? I'm indulging."

"That bad?" Root beer was Eddie's way of unwinding.

"Just long." He took a seat at the counter in front of his plate, put the root beers down, then twisted the cap off of one. "Mashed potatoes?"

"For you, yes."

"You really do love me."

"Yes, I do."

He took a sip of the soda then picked up his fork. "I had an early morning fishing trip, then back at ten to do a glass-bottom boat tour, which was really good. Katie and her son and his family all came. Sophie, Gage, and Owen, too. We saw a lot of sea life. That boat is going to be very popular."

"I'm sure." She went and sat beside him. She could smell the soap he'd used. His hair lay in damp curls around his neckline.

"Then the real fun started," he said. "Lala Queen and her crew showed up for a sunset cruise. I'd known they were coming, but I guess I didn't understand how much drama they were going to bring with them."

"So I've heard. What happened?"

He shook his head as he used the meatloaf on the end of his fork to scoop up some mashed potatoes. "It wasn't like there was any one thing, but that woman is...I don't know what she is. Half the time she was on her phone, the rest of the time she was asking questions, like why do dolphins live in the water if they need to breathe air and did I know that you can't eat fish if you're vegan?"

Olivia started laughing. "I can explain that one. Grace sent us all a group text about it. Apparently, she had to explain that to Lala at the restaurant tonight."

Eddie swallowed the bite he'd just taken. "How can the world make a celebrity out of that woman? Just because she can sing? And I'm not even sure about that. Her voice is probably autotuned."

"I have no idea, but she seems to be quite a handful. Traveling with as many people as she does means she's probably pretty well-insulated from real life."

He nodded. "I think that's right."

"You probably didn't have a chance to talk to anyone at Bluewater about a potential addition to the marina."

"Oh, no. I did that as soon as I could. I have three names. I just need to talk to them."

"Hire whichever one you like best."

He glanced at her. "You don't want to look at their resumes or talk to them yourself?"

She shook her head. "If you like them, that's good enough for me. Hire them soon, too. Like tomorrow."

"Tomorrow is Christmas Eve."

"So? I can't think of a better present than a job at Mother's."

He smiled. "Yeah, you're probably right. Okay, I'll take care of it. Thank you."

"You don't have to thank me. It's what the resort needs."

"True, but you could have said it wasn't in the budget."

"I would have found a way to make it happen. You and Rico are running yourselves ragged. Did you tell him about hiring another boat captain?"

"I mentioned it might happen. He was pretty happy."

"Good. Hopefully, you'll find someone who's a perfect fit." She rubbed his back. "I'm sorry about the long day."

"It's all good now. The shower and the dinner helped a lot." He looked at her. "But mostly it's being here with you."

She leaned against his shoulder, loving the warmth and strength that radiated off him. "You want to watch a Christmas movie? Or something?"

"Whatever you want is fine with me, so long as you

don't mind me falling asleep halfway through." He shrugged apologetically. "I'm pretty tired."

"Would you rather not do anything?"

"This is exactly where I want to be and what I want to be doing. Besides, you haven't even told me about your day yet."

"Ah. That. Well, long story short, Yolanda Oscott arrived today."

"*Ay caramba.*"

"Exactly." Olivia told him the long version, during which he shook his head a lot.

"Is Jenny okay?"

"She seems to be holding her own. No idea what happened after Leigh Ann and I left, but maybe Yolanda did some thinking."

"Maybe. Probably not."

"No, probably not. But hey, it's Christmas," Olivia said. "And if there was ever a time for miracles, this is it."

Chapter Twenty-five

Knowing things hadn't exactly gotten off to a great start with Yolanda, Iris had sent a text to Nick, inviting him, Jenny, and his mother to breakfast the next day. She'd cleared it with Vera first, who'd agreed right away, admitting she was eager to lay eyes on Yolanda.

Now, however, in the light of morning, Iris was regretting it a little. It was Christmas Eve day. A time of happiness and anticipation and last-minute preparations.

Yolanda felt like the last person anyone would want to spend time with on a day like this. But Iris couldn't exactly rescind her invitation. That would be a very Scroogey thing to do and she did not want to end up on Santa's naughty list.

She sat on the edge of the bed looking at Arthur's photo. "What did you ever see in that woman?"

But she knew exactly what he'd seen. It was clear

that once upon a time, many years ago, Yolanda had been a hot number. And men were easily swayed by a pretty face and curves in the right places. Even her sweet Arthur.

Iris hadn't been without her own charms, either, so it was mostly fortunate that men responded to such things.

Now, however, there was no undoing what she'd done. She had no choice but to get on with the day. She got up and went out for a cup of coffee and to see how Vera was doing with the preparations for breakfast.

The cats were out on the porch. Probably to keep them from getting underfoot, but none of them looked like they minded.

Iris understood Vera not wanting to deal with their begging. She was laying it on thick this morning and had a lot to accomplish. Fresh sausages from the best market in town, peppered bacon, sweet potato hash with onions, sage, and cranberries, and soft scrambled eggs flecked with chives. She was also putting out guava-orange juice, water, coffee, fruit salad, wheat toast, pumpkin muffins with cream cheese frosting, and a cheese plate. If Yolanda complained about this meal, she'd complain about anything.

Iris poured herself a cup of coffee. "It smells incredible in here. You're really setting out quite a spread."

"With that woman coming? You'd better believe it. I won't have her fussing about there not being enough to eat."

Iris felt pretty confident that Yolanda would find something to complain about all the same. "Anything I can do to help?"

Vera seemed lost in thought, her focus on the list in front of her. Then she shook her head. "Not that I can think of ... Wait. Would you set the table? I know that's not usually your job but—"

"Happy to help lighten the load," Iris said. She took her coffee with her to the table, where Vera already had put the dishes, silverware, and napkins. The fancy cloth ones, too.

Iris got everything all set, then went back for glasses and cups. This was going to be quite a meal. She wouldn't be indulging in all of it, though. She'd have the sausage and eggs, of course. And a little of the hash. Maybe a piece or two of fruit. But no toast or muffin. She wasn't going off her meal plan just because of Yolanda.

Iris wasn't about to sacrifice her health for anyone.

She put glasses and cups on the table, then went back to the kitchen. "Are you sure there isn't something else I can do?"

Vera glanced at the counter behind them. "You could pour that coffee into the carafe then start another pot. Other than that, just get yourself ready."

"I can do that." Iris hadn't made coffee in a long time, but she remembered how. Mostly. "Four scoops?"

"*Six* and a full pot of water."

"Got it." No wonder Vera's coffee was so strong, but Iris liked it that way. She got the machine going, then went off to take her shower.

She picked out a pretty caftan in pink and tropical green, which was sort of Christmassy in an island way.

When she got out of the shower, she dried her hair, put on lots of moisturizer, then penciled in her brows, dabbed on a little rouge, and even added a bit of lipstick. Not too much. She wasn't trying to beat Yolanda at her own game, just spruce up a smidge.

She went back out to the kitchen. Vera moved like a well-oiled machine, but then she'd been keeping house and looking after Iris and Arthur for years. This was her arena.

Vera pointed at a few things on the counter. "Butter, jam, sugar, and creamer can go on the table. Then you can fill the carafe the rest of the way and add that, too."

Iris grinned. Vera was truly in production mode. Iris did as she'd been told, arranging things as nicely as she could. She wished she'd had time to get a center-piece for the table, but there had to be something outside she could use.

She got a pair of kitchen shears from the drawer. "Be right back."

Out the door, down the steps and into the side yard

where all sorts of interesting foliage grew. She found exactly what she wanted in the tall hedge of variegated hibiscus. Not only were the leaves green and white, but the saucer-sized flowers were bright red.

She snipped a good bunch of them and carried them back upstairs. She arranged them in a small round glass vase with water and set them in the center of the table. They looked perfect. Just the right touch of green and red, and low enough not to impede conversation, which should be interesting, whatever the topic.

"Nicely done," Vera said.

"Thank you. I thought I should contribute something."

Vera laughed. "You've contributed plenty. My money didn't buy this food."

"No, but your hands prepared it and that's worth more."

Vera smiled just as someone knocked on the door.

"I'll get it," Iris said.

She opened it to find Nick, Yolanda, and Jenny standing there. "Happy Christmas Eve day."

"Happy Christmas Eve day to you," Nick said. "And thanks for inviting us."

"Yes," Jenny said. "That was so sweet of you."

Iris let them in. "Today is a day to be with friends and family."

Yolanda had yet to say anything.

"Morning," Vera called out. "Breakfast will be up in just a second. Have a seat and I'll bring it."

Iris nodded. "Help yourself to coffee and juice, too."

They all got seated. Yolanda on one side of Nick, Jenny on the other. Iris girded her loins and sat beside Yolanda.

She put on a bright smile. "How are you this morning?"

"Fine," Yolanda answered without any real inflection. If anything, she sounded tired.

"Any plans for the day?"

Yolanda shook her head. "I don't think so."

Iris looked at Nick as Vera brought a big bowl of the hash to the table. "You should see if Eddie has any open spots on the ten a.m. glass-bottom boat tour. That would be a lovely thing to do."

Nick's brows went up in question. "You wouldn't mind if we went on that?"

"Not at all. Not if Eddie has room." She understood why he'd ask. Iris had initially made it clear she didn't want Yolanda taking advantage of the amenities that were meant for resort guests, but it was nearly Christmas, and she couldn't imagine Nick and Jenny being cooped up with that woman all day.

Jenny smiled. "That would be great. Don't you think that sounds fun, Yolanda?"

Yolanda shrugged. "Sure."

Something was going on with her today. Iris just didn't know what.

Vera put the last of the dishes on the table, then took a seat beside Iris and began to pass them around. "Eat up. There's plenty more."

Yolanda made a face. "Your housekeeper eats with you?"

Iris nodded. "Vera isn't just my housekeeper, my caretaker, or my cook. She's my friend. A very dear one at that."

Yolanda just shook her head. A remarkably subdued reaction.

That only made Iris curiouser. "How was your evening yesterday? Did you all do anything?"

Nick glanced at Jenny. "The two of us went for a walk on the beach. My mother stayed in to read."

Yolanda helped herself to a scoop of hash. "A friend of mine has a book coming out next spring. She wanted me to review it for her."

"Isn't that nice," Iris said. "What kind of book is it?"

"A work of significant historical fiction," Yolanda answered.

"*The Rake's Revenge*," Nick said. "You should see the cover. Looks pretty racy."

Iris almost laughed, but Vera actually did.

She poured herself a small glass of juice. "Sounds like one of Katie's books."

"Katie, who lives on the second floor?" Yolanda asked.

Iris nodded. "Yes. She's a novelist. She writes as Iris Deveraux."

Yolanda looked at Jenny. "That's who you work for?"

"Yep," Jenny answered. "She's so nice."

Yolanda just sniffed and used her fork to push the food around on her plate. Then she shook her head. "I shouldn't have come here. It was a waste of my time. This place is crawling with...with...unsavory types."

Iris sniffed, but kept her takes-one-to-know-one comment to herself.

Nick put his fork down. "Mom, please. We talked about this last night. This is what I want to do with my life right now. This is where I want to be. There is nothing unsavory about this place or these people."

"They've turned you against me."

Vera's eyes narrowed. "I think you've done that yourself."

Anger flashed in Yolanda's eyes. "How dare you speak to me like that."

Iris wasn't having it. "Vera is right. You're pretty good at getting people to side with your son. You complain about everything. Nothing is good enough for you. Or for him, as far as you're concerned. I don't know why you think the world owes you something, but it doesn't. We're all just doing our best to find happiness and love. Why are you so against that?"

"Yeah," Vera said. "Who peed in your cornflakes?"

"I never." Yolanda stood up.

"Mom," Nick said. "Sit down. Or I will take you back to the airport myself today."

She stared at him, the color draining out of her face. Then she sat down. And started to cry.

Chapter Twenty-six

race slipped out of bed, pulled on her robe, put her feet into her slippers, then grabbed her phone off the nightstand and went downstairs. With her phone in her robe pocket, she went straight to the windows to look outside. They were open a little to let the fresh air in and it was wonderful.

She smiled. The sun seemed brighter, the sky bluer, the air perfectly crisp with just the right amount of salty tang. Maybe it felt that way because she had no work today or tomorrow. David did today, of course, because chefs rarely got a day off, although he would tomorrow, thanks to the rest of the kitchen crew and some careful planning.

The resort would be operating with minimal staffing for the next couple of days to give all of the employees extra time off. That had been made clear to guests long ago when they'd reserved Christmas week, but another reminder had been slipped beneath everyone's door last night.

Hopefully, the jovial spirit of Christmas would make everyone kind and understanding. She was thinking of Lala Queen in particular. But today was supposed to be a filming day, from what Grace understood of the young woman's schedule.

That should keep her busy. Although Grace wasn't sure how long a thing like that would last. Seemed like it might take all day.

Tonight, the resort was showing *It's A Wonderful Life* in the Treasures Pavilion where a special treat of Christmas cookies, hot chocolate, and eggnog would be served. The drinks would be available spiked, as well, but that didn't faze Grace one bit.

Tomorrow, all three meal services would only be offering a buffet. Boat service would be limited to staff requirements and emergencies.

Grace had shopped earlier in the week and was planning to do the cooking so that David really could rest. For breakfast, there would be pancakes, from a mix, but that was still sort of homemade. For during the day, she'd bought the supplies for a nice charcuterie board. A selection of cured meats, some salted nuts, great cheeses, different kinds of olives, some pickled vegetables, and some nice crackers and pita chips.

They could snack on that all day while they

lounged around and did nothing but enjoy each other's company.

For dinner, she had two filet mignons, which she knew David would insist on taking out to the grill. She was fine with that. She'd do the baked potatoes and creamed spinach. She'd bought a small key lime pie, too.

The day would be very laidback. Just the two of them, hanging out. Although they'd probably visit with the rest of the crew a bit. At least to do a little present exchange.

Whatever the day held, she was really looking forward to it. They'd worked hard these past ten months. Tomorrow's day of rest and togetherness had been well-earned.

She went into the kitchen and started a pot of coffee. She had a few presents to wrap. She'd gotten David a new robe. His current one was in a sad state. He said it was comfortable, but he could be just as comfortable in his new one, too. It was royal blue and super soft. She was sure he'd like it. And it didn't have any holes or bleach spots.

She'd gotten him some new chef pants, as well. And a nice pair of sunglasses. Those had come from the resort's gift shop, where she'd made good use of her employee discount. They were probably the most expensive thing she'd bought him in a long time, but she could afford it now, in part thanks to her OM coin investment.

But David deserved the best. Besides, living here meant he needed good eyewear.

For the girls and Iris, she'd gotten beautiful hand-made pottery mugs from Duke's mom's shop. Dixie had made them especially for Grace, putting the Delta Sigma letters on each one. Grace had put a nice bar of handmade soap into each mug. She'd found the soap in a shop in town. The fragrance was the most delicious smelling frangipani, which was another name for the sweet-smelling plumeria that grew all over the place.

Her mind went back to Christmas Day and being able to spend time with David.

She was hoping that as things progressed with Phase II and the hiring of more staff, he'd be able to take a little more time off and do some of that fishing he always talked about. Both Grant and Duke had offered to take him. Eddie, too.

Maybe they could all go. Might be a nice bonding experience for the guys. She made a mental note to talk to the rest of the girls about setting that up. She'd ask Katie if Owen would be interested.

The coffeemaker sputtered as it finished brewing. She went to get herself a cup, added a little cream and a couple drops of her favorite sugar-free liquid sweet-ener, then went out to sit on the front porch.

The view was so perfect, she took a snapshot and posted it to her social media, tagging the resort and using the hashtags #ChristmasonCompassKey and #ChristmasatMothers. That should make Katie and Jenny happy. The two had been working hard to get the resort's name out there a little more.

Like all of them, they were concerned that Phase II be well received. There was a lot of money at stake, but that wasn't the only reason they wanted it to be successful. The success of that new area would color their futures.

She tucked her phone away and sipped her coffee, feeling a deep sense of contentment. Life was so good. Even things with Curt had worked out.

She was almost to the bottom of her cup when David joined her, a mug of his own in hand.

"Morning, sweetheart."

"Morning." She smiled up at him. There was something so endearing about his messy hair right after he woke up. "How'd you sleep?"

"Good. You?" He sat beside her.

"Great. Beautiful day, huh?"

"It is. But then, it almost always is. I hope I never take that for granted."

She shook her head. "I don't think this view will ever get old."

"Me either."

They sat in silence for a while until her phone

vibrated. She pulled it from her pocket and checked the screen.

"Who is it?"

She read the name. "Curt." She tapped the notification. "It's a group text. He sent it to you, too."

"My phone's still upstairs. Read it to me?"

She nodded. "Sorry to bother you on Christmas Eve, but my apartment complex has had a water main break. My first-floor apartment is flooded. They don't expect to have it repaired for at least a week. Is there any availability at the resort?"

She looked at David. "That's awful. I feel bad for Curt, but I feel bad for everyone who lives there. No water for Christmas? I hope he can salvage some of his stuff."

David made a face. "What a time of year for it to happen. I bet there's nothing available for miles around."

A second text came through. She read it. "I've called a bunch of hotels and they're all booked, otherwise I wouldn't ask."

She sighed in her husband's direction. "You must be psychic." She stared at her screen. "Amanda would know for sure, but I'm positive the whole resort is booked. Lala and her group took almost half of it themselves."

David sipped his coffee before speaking again. "We do have a guest room."

She raised her brows. "We do, but would you really be okay with Curt staying here?"

"I wouldn't suggest it if I wasn't, but the real question is, would *you* be okay with it? You're the one who has history with him."

She shrugged. "I feel like that's been dealt with about as much as it can be. But having him here would mean our day off together tomorrow would be a little interrupted."

"I know," David said. "I guess that's really what I was asking when I wanted to know if you'd be okay with it. I mean with all of it. It's up to you."

She appreciated David letting her make the decision, but she also knew that Curt was the guy they needed to manage the two new eateries. He was better qualified than anyone else who'd applied. By leaps and bounds. She also knew how important it was for David to have the peace of mind that the person they'd given that job to would be available. They needed Curt. The resort needed him.

And the resort prided itself on taking care of its employees.

"It's okay," she said. "He can stay here. Where else is he going to go?" She picked up her phone to answer.

"Hang on," David said. "Are you sure? I know we're relying on him to fill a pretty important role. But I don't want to do this if it means it ruins something between us."

She smiled, touched by his concern. "It's not going to ruin anything between us. There will be other Christmases and other days off. Especially once Curt's on board. We can still do some things by ourselves tomorrow. A walk on the beach maybe? We'll figure it out. If there was ever a time to extend a helping hand, it's Christmas."

David reached over to touch her arm. "I love you. You have a great heart, you know that? I promise I'll make this up to you."

"You don't need to make it up to me."

"Yeah," he said. "I do."

Still smiling, she texted Curt back, reading the words out loud as she typed them. "You can stay in our guest room. Not sure about getting you a ride here. Need to check with the boat captains."

She turned toward David. "What do you think?"

"Sounds good to me." He set his cup down. "I'll be right back."

"Okay." She hit Send.

It would be a little weird to have Curt staying with them, but only at first. And it would be a great chance for David to get to know the man who'd be working for him. For them.

David returned with a small wrapped gift in his hand. He held it out to her. "For you."

"Now?"

"Why not?"

She grinned and took the present. Her phone went off again, but so did David's and he had his with him now.

He read the message. "Curt says thank you so much. I am eternally grateful. I'll pack a bag right now." David glanced over. "What should I tell him about getting ferried over?"

"Tell him I'll send a time for him to be at Bluewater Marina after I talk to the boat captains."

David typed the message in, then hit Send. "Done." He put the phone down. "Now open your gift."

Still smiling, she unwrapped the package. As soon as the paper was off, she knew it was jewelry. She couldn't imagine what. She opened the hinged box and took a breath. "Diamond earrings? These look really expensive."

The diamond studs were about the diameter of pencil erasers, maybe bigger, and flashed with all kinds of sparkle. They were gorgeous. She shook her head. "You shouldn't have spent so much."

"Okay, listen," he said. "For one thing, you deserve them. Remember when you pawned your diamond studs to help us open our first restaurant? I always said I'd get you another pair when we could afford it, and now we can."

"But—"

"For another thing, I used the advance from the cookbook. And for a third thing, those also came from a pawn shop, so I got a really good deal. They're ninety points apiece, so not quite a carat each. Biggest and nicest they had."

The ones she'd pawned years ago had only been half a carat each. These were a big step up. She couldn't believe what he'd done. Still holding the box, she got up and sat on his lap to hug him. "Thank you."

He held her close, kissing her temple. "Merry Christmas, Gracie."

Chapter Twenty-seven

*L*eigh Ann got Rita through her workout, then pretty much ran back to her bungalow to change and put on a little makeup before going to see Grant at his studio.

Right after agreeing to paint Lala as a mermaid, he'd decided the best thing for him to do was work as much as possible for as long as it took to get the painting done. He'd been crashing at her place, which she didn't mind at all, but he hadn't come in until after eleven last night and when she'd gotten up to get ready for Rita's six a.m. yoga, he'd already been gone.

She'd seen so little of him these past two days and she didn't like it.

But she also had herself to blame. She'd pushed him to accept the commission because she'd wanted to keep Lala happy and stop her from potentially giving the resort any bad press. Grant could have said no, of course, but she knew he'd agreed in part because she'd wanted him to.

Sure, Lala was paying him a stupid amount of money, but Grant was doing fine all on his own. He didn't really need Lala's check.

Now, guilt hung over Leigh Ann like a gloomy cloud. She was determined to make it up to him by doing whatever he needed done. Even if that meant going to his house on the mainland and cleaning it. Or whatever.

She was also taking him breakfast. Toasted bagels with cream cheese, protein yogurt with fruit and granola on the side to add in, ham and cheese rollups, plus a thermos of strong coffee and two bottles of coconut water. She packed it all up in a rolling cooler, then carried it down the steps and headed for his studio.

There was no way he was working tomorrow. It was Christmas, for Pete's sake. She was hoping to see the girls, exchange gifts, then spend most of the day just being with Grant. They'd talked about going out on his boat for a little cruise, but not doing too much more.

She had a feeling that was the plan for most of the girls. A down day spent with their significant others, just enjoying the time off. They'd all been working so hard. A real day off would be such a gift.

She rolled the cooler behind her, enjoying the morning. It was still very early, but the workers were already on site at both the new staff bungalows and at Phase II. Her first thought was for Eddie and Rico, the two men responsible for ferrying those workers in.

How early had they gotten up?

The whole resort crew needed some time off. Which would be happening this whole week, but tomorrow especially.

She went past Phase II and on down the path that led toward Grant's studio. The marina was visible, as was Eddie on the pontoon. She waved at him. He waved back. No sign of Rico, so she figured he was either doing an early morning fishing trip or bringing more workers, possibly resort employees, in.

They really needed another boat captain, but Leigh Ann knew that was being worked on. She also wondered how Yolanda's stay was going.

But she was at the studio now, and her attention belonged to Grant. The big garage door was open.

Grant was inside, sitting in one of the tall director's chairs, brush in hand doing what looked like fine detail work.

She stayed by the door. She wasn't sure he wasn't a little mad at her for pushing him to do this. "Morning," she said softly.

He turned, saw her, and smiled. "Morning, beautiful."

She took a few steps in. He didn't seem mad. "I hope I'm not bothering you."

"Never."

She went closer. "Tell me the truth. Are you mad at me for getting you into this?"

His brows went up. "You mean painting Lala's portrait? Why would I be mad at you for a decision I made?"

"Because I pushed you to do it."

He put his brush down on his worktable and held out his hand. "Come here."

She walked to him, still rolling the cooler behind her.

He put his arm around her and kissed her mouth. "The decision was mine. Yes, you encouraged me, but you were right to do it."

She leaned back. "I was?"

"Of course. Do you realize how much press this will get me? I know it might just be a fifteen-minute burst, but I'm okay with that. I can make that fifteen minutes work for me. My gallery crew is primed and ready. I already have some temporary help on standby. And this will be good for the resort, too."

She nodded, exhaling in relief. "I'm so glad. I've been feeling bad about this and—"

"Please don't. There is nothing for you to feel bad about." He smiled at her. "I'm a grown man. I could have just as easily said no."

"But you didn't."

"Would you have said no to half a million dollars?"

She smiled. "No." She rubbed his arm. "But you've been working so much lately."

"Because I want to get this painting *done*. Partially because I'm eager to return to my new work, but also because Lala doesn't strike me as someone who will want to wait."

"I agree with you there," Leigh Ann said. "How's it coming?"

He nodded at the canvas. "See for yourself."

Still in his arms, she turned to face the canvas. "Oh, wow. You've done a lot."

The painting was really coming to life. Lala, easily recognizable, sat on a throne of coral and shells underwater. Tiny fish swam past in two glittering schools and in the background, dolphins and sea turtles drifted by. Another small school of fish circled overhead, creating the illusion that she was wearing a crown.

Lala would love that, Leigh Ann thought.

She studied the rest of the painting. Lala was, as requested, a pink mermaid, but Grant had added some shimmery pearlescence to the tail as well. Her hair wasn't braided but instead flowed around her in soft blond and pink waves, accented with what looked like jewels but were actually tiny starfish, sea urchins, and strands of pearls.

The painting was remarkably detailed for him only having worked on it for two days. Sure, he'd worked a lot of hours in those two days, but still.

She shook her head. "How on Earth did you get this much done already?"

"I'll tell you a secret if you promise to keep it between us."

She smiled and made the motions to go along with her words. "Cross my heart and hope to die."

"This is an old canvas that I started a couple years ago and never finished because I wasn't happy with it. Much like the painting I was working on when I met you, it was one of those where the woman in the midst of it never felt right. I couldn't capture her. This felt like the right opportunity to finally give it a home."

"That was smart," Leigh Ann said. "Lala's going to love this."

"You think so?"

She nodded. "From what I've seen of her, this seems to be right up her alley. Maybe not enough glitter or sparkle, but she can't expect that from a painting."

"Actually..." Grant said. He reached over to his worktable and picked up a small, lidded jar. "I'm going to add some of this when I'm done. As an accent."

He twisted the top off and showed Leigh Ann the inside. Tiny iridescent dust suspended in a milky gel-like substance. "It dries clear," he said. "Leaving only the whisper of light behind. It's a micro glitter. I bought it years ago thinking I would use it for some stars in one of my paintings, but the effect was a little too velvet Elvis for me."

She laughed. "Velvet Elvis. You're funny. But I bet Lala thinks it's, like, the bomb. Or whatever kids say these days."

He nodded as he put the top back on. "Let's hope so."

"Hey, are you able to take a little break?" She tipped her head toward the cooler at her feet. "I brought breakfast."

"That sounds perfect. And much better than the protein bars I was going to have."

"Come on," she said. "You've earned it."

"Any chance you have coffee in there?"

"I do. A whole thermos full."

"I love you."

She grinned. "I love you, too."

She went to work unpacking the cooler and setting everything out on the tall pub table where he usually ate his lunch.

He brought his chair over, along with two mugs, and sat with her.

She poured coffee for him. "You're not working tomorrow, you know."

"I'm not?"

"No. It's Christmas. You're spending it with me. Doing Christmas Day things."

"Which are?" He grinned, clearly enjoying this.

"Having an indulgent breakfast, opening presents, visiting with—"

"Opening presents?" His look of pretend shock wasn't very convincing. "Was I supposed to get you something?"

She shook her head at his teasing. "You know Owen got Katie a boat."

He nodded, smiling like the cat who'd caught the canary. "I know. He asked my opinion about it. Pretty nice gift. Is that what you're hoping for? A boat?"

"I don't need anything that elaborate." She'd gotten him a beautiful glass starfish. They'd seen it together at a craft fair at the end of summer. It was all handmade and filled with the most vibrant colors. He'd loved it on sight but hadn't been able to decide whether or not to spend the money.

A few minutes after they'd left the craftswoman's table, Leigh Ann had made an excuse to slip away, gone back and purchased it.

During lunch at the fair, Grant had finally decided to buy the piece. Of course, when they'd gone back, the starfish was marked Sold.

He'd been so disappointed. Leigh Ann had barely kept herself from telling him the truth right then. Christmas Day was going to be fun.

He sipped his coffee. "I have something for you I think you're going to like."

"Is that so?" she said. "I have the same sort of gift for you."

"Do you?" He looked interested. "What's that?"

"Nope." She just shook her head and smiled. She wasn't about to let the secret slip after this many months.

Chapter Twenty-eight

Amanda had only worked the front counter by herself once before. She wasn't too nervous, though. She'd been working at the resort for plenty of time now and today would be a light day. After all, there was no one checking in or out.

It was the perfect day for Carissa to have off.

And not just because Lala Queen and her group were out filming on a boat today.

There wasn't a whole lot for Amanda to do except wait for the phone to ring and help any guests that might come by.

People would be coming to The Palms soon for breakfast. She imagined that would get her a few guests who needed something.

She drank her coffee, glad she'd gotten a cup. She had a bottle of water with her, too. For lunch, she'd get a salad from The Palms. Maybe the mahi mahi Caesar.

Not that she was hungry. She'd made herself scrambled eggs and sausage this morning. She heard the doors open, a sure sign that guests were coming for breakfast. She put a smile on her face, ready to greet whoever might come by.

A couple approached the front desk. She recognized them instantly. Michael Gideon and Kit Tellman, the Hollywood couple who'd come here in hopes of rekindling their rocky marriage.

Amanda went on alert, wondering what they needed. Then she saw they were holding hands. That was a good sign, wasn't it?

She broadened her smile. "Good morning."

"Morning," Michael said. "We were just talking on the way into breakfast, and we were wondering if you could set up another of those couple's massages for us? Tomorrow, if possible. Which I realize is Christmas Day, but we're willing to pay overtime for the massage therapists, if necessary."

Amanda nodded. "I will see if I can make that happen for you." They must have really enjoyed the first one. "If not tomorrow, would the 26th work?"

Kit smiled. At her husband. "The 26th would be fine, although tomorrow would be extra special." She looked at Amanda. "Did one of our assistants set us up with the honeymoon package? Are you able to find that out? I'd like to say thank you to whichever one of them did it. Such a nice surprise."

Amanda wasn't sure what was protocol, but telling the truth seemed all right. Or at least a close proximity. "That was actually me. I confess that I knew you'd just gotten married this summer and as you were first-time guests to Mother's, I wanted to do something special for you."

Kit laughed. "That was a very kind thing for you to do. We really enjoyed the champagne and chocolate-covered strawberries." She leaned against Michael. "And the couple's massage. Obviously."

Michael kissed Kit's cheek. "Yeah, it was great. This whole trip has been great. I'd be happy to tell your manager what a nice thing you did for us. If that would help you at all."

Amanda shook her head, so pleased things were going well for the newlywed couple. "I'm one of the owners of the resort, but I appreciate the feedback all the same. And I am so happy to hear you're having a good time. I'll find out about that massage and get back to you as soon as I know."

Kit put her hand flat on the countertop. "Thank you again."

"You're welcome. Enjoy your breakfast."

They walked away, arm in arm, looking very much like a couple in love.

Amanda would have to do something nice for Carissa. Maybe get her a little housewarming gift for when she moved on property. After all, Carissa had pointed Michael and Kit's reservation out to Amanda. She wouldn't have known about them otherwise.

She pulled up the incoming reservations page on the computer in front of her. Some of the names were familiar, some weren't. Returning guests were marked with one code, first-timers with another. But that was about it.

If the guest had requested to celebrate a specific occasion while at the resort, that was in their notes section.

But the rest of the special information about the guests, like what Carissa had told her, seemed to reside primarily in Carissa's head. She was the one who took a lot of the reservations, but Amanda was doing more and more of that now.

Maybe anything special should be added to the notes section, too. But Amanda could see how that might not work out as planned, either. She was sure neither Michael nor Kit would have liked knowing that their failing marriage had been a topic of staff discussion. Finding out a note about it had been added to their file could prove disastrous for the resort if it ever got out.

Everyone who worked here was supposed to be the soul of discretion, even signing paperwork to that effect, but there was always a chance someone wouldn't adhere to that. Or that a guest might accidentally see something.

Either way, putting those kinds of details in writing seemed like a potentially bad idea, no matter the original good intention.

But she put a pin in that idea for the moment. Right now, she needed to know if she could set Michael and Kit up with another couple's massage on Christmas Day. She wasn't so sure she could make that happen.

She decided to start with the woman in charge of the spa. Leigh Ann.

Amanda sent her a text. *Are you busy? I have a spa question.*

Leigh Ann's answer came quickly. *Eating breakfast with Grant. What's the question?*

Any chance there are two massage therapists available to do a couple's massage tomorrow?

On Christmas? Not sure. I'll need to look at the schedule and see who's on and if there are any appointments open.

They're willing to pay extra, Amanda added, just in case it might help.

Good to know.

A couple of minutes later, Leigh Ann texted back. *Do they have a preference for male or female massage therapists?*

They didn't say. I'd guess no preference.

Okay.

Amanda went back to waiting. She helped a couple who needed more shampoo. Took a call from someone wanting to know if they had any availability for the week of New Year's, which they didn't, and got an older man some more hangers.

Finally, Leigh Ann texted again. *Can they do two pm?*

I'm sure they could.

Done deal. It'll be an extra $300. But you need to make sure either Rico or Eddie can ferry the MTs to the resort then back to the marina.

Amanda hadn't thought about that. She hated to make more people work on Christmas Day. She wondered if Michael and Kit knew how big of an ask this couple's massage was. Or maybe being a celebrity meant they didn't think about things like that?

She sent Rico and Eddie a joint text. *I hate to ask but can either of you pick up two massage therapists at 1:30 tomorrow, then take them back around 3?*

Maybe she should just set it up for the 26th, but she really wanted to make this happen for Michael and Kit. She didn't want anything to interrupt the island magic or Christmas magic or whatever it was that was bringing them back together again. There was something so wonderful about the chance to be part of that.

Eddie responded first. *I can bring them in if Rico can take them back.*

Rico's response showed up next. *I can't. I'm headed to my parents in Fort Lauderdale in the morning. Sorry.*

Amanda racked her brain for a solution. Katie had a boat now. Maybe she could do it? Or maybe Grant? Then it hit her. Duke. They'd be going to the mainland anyway to go to his parents.

She texted him. *Can we take two massage therapists back to the mainland around 3 tomorrow? I was thinking we were headed there anyway.*

She knew it might take him a minute to check his phone, so she busied herself with straightening up the already neat desk.

A woman came by. A familiar woman. Rita Harlow. She smiled as she approached. "Good morning."

"Good morning, Ms. Harlow. How can I help you?"

She slid a square envelope across the counter. It had Leigh Ann's name written on it. "I'd like to leave this for Leigh Ann Durham. Can you be sure she gets it?"

"I'll put it in her mailbox now."

"Thank you."

"You're welcome." Amanda took the envelope. Felt like a Christmas card. That was nice. "Is there anything else I can help you with?"

"No, that's all. Have a good day."

"You, too."

As Rita Harlow went toward The Palms, Amanda's phone rang. It was Duke. She answered with a smile. "Good morning."

"Morning. I was getting coffee and thought it might be easier to call. We can take people back tomorrow, that's not a problem but I can take them back today if they need to go sooner. I could run them to the marina after I get off. I'll be done by one today, because we're only working a half day."

"Thank you. It has to be tomorrow, though. I have guests who really want a couple's massage tomorrow, so I was trying to work out the logistics."

"Let me guess. Celebrities?"

"Yes." She looked around to make sure no one could overhear. She didn't like talking about guests, but this was a special situation. "It's Michael Gideon and Kit Tellman."

"*The* Michael Gideon? The action star guy."

"Yep, that's him."

"Oh, man. I don't usually do this, but I've been kinda stuck on a gift for my dad. I ended up getting him Michael's book. Do you think you could get him to sign it for my dad? He would love that."

Amanda smiled. "I'm sure I can. Where's the book?"

"In my bungalow, but I will go get it right now and bring it to you if that helps."

"It would. I can't leave here, since I'm the only one on duty."

"I'm on my way. Thank you."

"Happy to do it." She was pretty sure Michael

would be, too, after she explained how Duke was helping out.

But that was how Christmas worked, wasn't it? All sorts of wonderful, kind, unexpected things happened. At least, Amanda thought, for other people.

Chapter Twenty-nine

Dakota had talked about the glass-bottom boat ride so much that Katie had set up a second one as a surprise for Christmas Eve day.

Katie and her crew arrived en masse at the marina almost exactly at ten, a feat she felt deserved some applause, considering how much coordination that had taken. From the looks of it, they were also the first ones there.

Eddie gave her a wave. "Morning, Katie."

"Morning, Eddie. Thanks for taking us again." She already planned on giving him a fat tip for this.

Owen helped Katie onto the glass-bottom boat then made way for Josh and his family.

Eddie greeted them all. "Welcome aboard, folks." He waved at Dakota, who was wearing a princess dress and tiara this morning, having dressed herself. Eddie bowed. "It's a pleasure to have you on board again, your highness."

Dakota giggled. "I'm not a real princess."

Eddie acted very surprised. "You look like one to me."

"I wanna see *dophins*."

Eddie put his hand over his heart. "I am going to do my best, your highness." With Christy's help, he got Dakota and Gunner fitted for life vests.

While they worked on that, Katie and Owen took seats at one end, leaving the middle seats for Josh, Christy, and the kids. Not that Gunner would remember any of this. Sophie and Gage got on last and also went to the end of the boat.

The boat was a wide, open craft with a roof that covered the entire thing. The roof was necessary to keep the sun off the center strip of glass, otherwise the glare would have made it impossible to see through. A metal railing surrounded the glass strip, making sure no one stepped on it, although Eddie had told the girls on their first trip that the glass was very thick and could withstand being stood on. It still wasn't recommended, obviously.

Another couple approached the boat, an older couple. Mid- to late sixties, Katie thought.

She hoped they didn't mind that there were children aboard. Mother's was generally considered a kid-free resort, although that would be changing when Phase II opened. They were already preparing for it, which was why the boat was equipped with life jackets for the kids. There were more in the marina's office, too.

But the couple smiled when they saw Dakota. The older woman waved at her.

Dakota took the opening. "I'm not a real princess," she announced.

The older woman laughed. "Are you sure? You certainly look like a real princess."

Dakota suddenly got shy and ran back to Christy.

Laughing, the older couple sat across from Josh and Christy on the other side.

Eddie addressed them. "Welcome aboard, everyone. I'm your captain, Eddie Cabrera. We had a few cancellations, so this is all of us, which means we'll be heading out now. Keep your eyes on the glass. You never know what might show up."

He untied the boat and accelerated slightly as they left the marina behind. The breeze drifted over them, tangy with salt. Katie inhaled deeply, loving the day already.

The older man glanced at Owen, eyes narrowing like he'd just realized who he was sharing company with.

Owen took notice, giving him a nod. "Merry Christmas."

"Merry Christmas," the man said. "I'm Chuck Hartman."

Owen smiled. "I thought you looked familiar. Owen Monk."

Chuck smiled. "I know who you are."

Owen patted Katie's leg. "This is my fiancée and one of the resort's owners, Katie Walchech, and her family. Katie, this is Chuck Hartman and his wife, Dolores. Chuck owns the San Antonio Predators. The hockey team."

"Oh, right," Katie said. She'd heard of them, but that was about as far as her knowledge of the team went. "Nice to meet you both." She pointed to Sophie. "This is my sister, Sophie, Owen's head of security, Gage, my son, Josh, his wife, Christy, and that's Gunner in her arms and Princess Dakota you've met."

Chuck and his wife nodded, greeting the rest of them.

Katie laughed. "Don't worry, there won't be a quiz."

Josh looked a little starstruck. "I love the Predators. You've got a great team. LaForge and Ward are two of the best players on the ice today."

Chuck smiled. "I'd tend to agree with you there. Have you been to a game?"

Josh shook his head reluctantly. "Not yet. Maybe someday. I'm a teacher, so my schedule is a little tight during the season."

Probably his budget was a little tight, too. Katie didn't know how much hockey tickets cost, but weren't all professional sports expensive events to attend?

"Teaching is an admirable profession," Chuck said. "If you ever want to come to a game, you let me know. You can come as my guest. Just give me a call." He dug a business card from his pocket and handed it over.

"Wow, thanks," Josh said as he took the card. "That would be amazing."

"Fishes!" Dakota announced then with such excitement everyone stopped talking to look.

Eddie smiled. "We're moving over a shallow area right now where you'll see a lot of small fish, some upside-down jellies, and possibly a baby shark or even a stingray. This area is commonly considered a nursery, because so many fish have their young here."

Owen kissed Katie's cheek, making her smile. "Doing this again was a great idea."

"Thanks. Dakota sure seems to be having fun."

He laughed. "Dakota has fun everywhere."

"True."

Christy leaned forward with Gunner in her arms.

Katie held out her hands. "Why don't you let me take him so you can see better?"

"Are you sure?"

"I would be happy to. And when my arms get tired, his Aunt Sophie can take over."

Sophie nodded, grinning. "All day, any day."

Christy passed Gunner to Josh, who passed him to Katie. She held him on her lap so he faced out. Under his life vest, he was in a little white onesie printed with navy anchors, soft, knit jeans, white socks, and a white bucket hat, which did nothing to stop Katie from inhaling that unique baby scent of his.

Everyone was watching the glass, but Dakota was sitting by the railing around the glass now, pointing out every fish that swam under the boat.

Katie was so happy she could have cried. How had this magical existence become her life? Eddie turned the boat slightly, sending a ray of sun over her engagement ring and making it flash with a rainbow of colors.

This life was so beyond description that she wasn't sure even she had enough words for how blessed she felt.

Owen put his arm around her.

She took a deep breath and settled against him, bouncing Gunner ever so slightly. She watched Dakota, mesmerized by the little girl's unbridled enthusiasm. Her granddaughter. Who was also going to be her flower girl.

Life really didn't get any better.

She smiled at Owen. Okay, maybe being Owen's wife would take things up a notch, but other than that, she couldn't imagine needing anything more out of life than what she had right now.

Chapter Thirty

Jenny didn't know what to do. Since Yolanda had broken down at Iris's and then run off back to Nick's, the older woman had been walking around the house like a zombie. When she actually left her room, that was.

Nick had tried to talk to his mother when she'd been sitting out on the porch, staring off at the water, but she'd just gotten up and gone back to her room, closing the door.

Nick had said they should just let her be. That this was a manipulation tactic.

But Jenny had her doubts about that. In a weird way, she not only felt for Yolanda, but she kind of understood what she was going through.

When Jenny and her mom had been estranged, that moment when Jenny had realized how wrong she'd been about her mom had been like a slap in the face. She'd had to take her own measure and accept that her bad attitude and hard feelings were her own doing. And most of what was causing the problem in the first place.

It had been a pretty sobering chapter of her life. And not a little humiliating. She'd done some serious soul searching and it hadn't been fun.

She had a feeling that was what Yolanda was going through now after seeing what Nick's life here was really like.

Nick came out of the bedroom. "I have to run to the office. A guest got a fishhook in their hand."

She made a face. "That doesn't sound like fun."

"Not at all. I'll be back as soon as I can."

"No rush." She leaned up to give him a kiss.

"See you later."

"Later." As she watched him leave, she made a determination. She was going to talk to Yolanda. Things couldn't get much worse, so Jenny didn't see a lot of downside.

She fixed two cups of coffee, one for herself, one for Yolanda, trying to remember how the woman took it. Then she carried them to Yolanda's room. "Yolanda? It's Jenny. I brought you some coffee."

There was no answer, but Jenny hadn't expected one. She tried a different tactic. Brutal honesty.

"My mom and I were estranged for a long time. She

made a lot of bad choices. Or so I thought. When I finally realized what the problem was, turned out it was me. My attitude. My expectations. My own willful ignorance." It had also been some lies her father had told her, but if she'd been willing to open her eyes sooner she would have seen the truth for herself.

Still no response but Jenny wasn't giving up. "It took a lot of self-searching and a serious amount of personal humiliation for me to make things right. I owed my mom the kind of apology that left me feeling bruised. It was hard to admit what a fool I'd been. But now we have a great relationship. One we could have had years ago, if only…"

Jenny sighed at the still closed door. Maybe this was a waste of breath. Maybe she should just go lose herself in work and—

The door opened a crack and Yolanda stood there, looking very much like she'd been crying again.

Jenny held up the coffee she'd made for her. "Want your coffee?"

"I don't think he'll forgive me."

"Of course he will. He would love to have a better relationship with you. He just doesn't think there's any way to make that happen, so I think he's given up a little."

Yolanda took a deep, shuddering breath.

"You can change that, though."

"I don't think so."

"I do." Jenny pushed the coffee at her, forcing Yolanda to open the door and take it.

Yolanda stared at Jenny with a lot of suspicion in her eyes. But she took the coffee. "Why are you being so nice to me?"

"Because you're a human being. And like I said, I've been where you are. I know what it feels like. But I also know you can get through it and come out the other side with a whole new outlook on life. You just have to do the work."

Yolanda focused on the cup in her hands. "I don't know how."

"Neither did I until I just did it."

Yolanda looked up. "How?"

Jenny smiled. "Why don't you come out and let me make us some breakfast and we can talk?"

Yolanda hesitated. "I should take a shower."

"And then we can talk?"

After a moment, Yolanda nodded. "Okay."

"Eggs and toast all right for breakfast?"

"Sure. Thank you. I thought you hated me."

"Me?" Jenny was surprised by that.

"I thought everyone did."

"More likely they're just put off by your attitude."

Yolanda exhaled. "Yeah."

"Go shower. I'll get some scrambled eggs and toast going and we'll have that talk."

"Okay. Thank you for the coffee. And for...wanting to help."

"You're welcome." Jenny took her coffee back to the kitchen and got to work on the food. Her mom and her friends were always saying this island had its own kind of magic. Maybe they were right.

She got eggs, butter, and the loaf of wheat bread from the fridge, along with a jar of guava jam that Nick had really been into lately. They'd had grapefruit marmalade the month before. He loved trying all the tropical flavors. Maybe his mom would like it, too.

She popped four slices of bread into the toaster's slots but didn't push the levers down to turn the machine on yet.

Next, she got a bowl, a fork, and a pan. She put butter in the pan and set it on a medium-heat burner. She cracked six eggs into the bowl, adding a little water, and whipped them up with the fork.

As much as she would have liked to add some veggies or something else, this didn't feel like the breakfast to get too ambitious with. She pushed the toaster levers down.

By the time she was just about done with the eggs, Yolanda came out, wearing a robe. Her hair was wrapped in a towel and there wasn't a stitch of makeup on her face. She looked a lot younger.

But also a little scared. Or maybe hopeless was a better description.

She put her cup on the counter.

"Would you like some more coffee?" Jenny asked.

Yolanda nodded. "Yes. But I can get it."

The toast popped up. "Breakfast is about ready. Why don't we eat on the porch? It's a beautiful day. Especially considering it's Christmas Eve."

"Okay." Yolanda's face remained nearly expressionless. She still seemed very much like a woman trapped in her own bleak thoughts. She shuffled over to the coffeemaker and refilled her cup.

Jenny got the toast buttered, then put two pieces on each plate and started portioning out the eggs.

"Is there anything I can do to help?"

Jenny looked up with a smile. "Sure. Can you take the jam and a butter knife out to the table?"

Yolanda nodded and did as Jenny had asked. Jenny followed with the two plates, silverware clutched in her hands as well. She set the plates down, then went back in for her coffee. She warmed it up by added a little more.

Yolanda was already seated when she came back. Jenny sat next to her. "Have you ever tried guava jam? Nick really likes it."

"No," Yolanda said. She stared at the jar, but Jenny wasn't so sure she was really looking at it.

"You could start with an apology," Jenny said softly. "I know that would go a long way with Nick. He really does love you. And I know he'd love to have a better relationship with you."

"What do I apologize for?"

Jenny picked up her fork. "You need to answer that. You need to take a hard look at how things have been between you, then figure that out. That's what I had to do."

Yolanda picked up the jam and the knife and began to spread some on her toast. "I've been too hard on him. Too demanding. Too critical. I knew it at the time, but I couldn't stop myself. I told myself I was being helpful. Guiding him."

She put the jam and the knife down and looked toward the water. "I'm like that with everyone. And I don't know why."

"Was your mom like that?"

Yolanda made eye contact with Jenny then. "No. My mother was a pushover. I watched my father walk all over her for years."

"So..." Jenny held her words, thinking they might be better off unsaid.

"What?"

Jenny shook her head. "I shouldn't—"

"Say it."

"You take after your father then."

Yolanda stared at her. Then slowly started to nod. "I guess I do. I never thought about that until now. I'm as bad as he was. Maybe worse."

The door opened and Nick walked in. He came straight out to join them. "Hey."

"Hi." Jenny could see the questions and confusion on his face.

Yolanda took a deep breath. "Nick? Could we talk?"

Chapter Thirty-one

Olivia was enjoying her day off. Which wasn't to say she hadn't done some work. She had. She'd run a report as part of her overview of the spa and its sales. But then she'd come back to her bungalow and done something she hadn't done in years.

She'd gotten busy baking Christmas cookies. She'd bought some tins and planned to take them around to some of the other employees tonight.

She was making three kinds. Snowballs, peanut butter kisses, and sugar cookies sprinkled with red and green sugar. If she got them done faster than anticipated, she was thinking about adding a pan of Toll House cookie bars with toffee pieces.

The television was playing her favorite fireplace channel, filling the house with the crackle of the fire and the soft sounds of Christmas music. The windows were open, letting in the breeze and the sweet smells of the flowers.

But the kitchen was generating its own sweet smells, too.

She couldn't remember a time when she'd had a nicer Christmas. She was just filled with the holiday spirit and so happy.

She started singing along as *White Christmas* played, which almost made her miss the knock on her door.

She wiped her hands on her apron and went to answer it.

Jenny was on the other side. "Hi, Mom. You look busy."

"Hi, honey. I'm making Christmas cookies."

"For real? Wow. No wonder it smells so good in here."

"Come on in. You want some coffee?"

"No, I'm good." Jenny had a curious look on her face as she came inside. "I just had breakfast with Yolanda."

Olivia cringed. "How did that go?"

"You're not going to believe this, but she and Nick are back at the house having a serious heart to heart about...well, their relationship."

Olivia's mouth came open. "How did that happen?"

The oven buzzer went off. Olivia threw her hands up. "The snowballs! I have to get them out."

"Go on," Jenny said, laughing. "It's so Christmassy in here. And you're like one of Santa's elves."

Olivia laughed too as she got the cookies out and started transferring them to a rack to cool. "I hope I'm as fast as one. Go on, back to Yolanda and Nick."

"I decided to talk to her this morning. Tell her a little about you and me. Mostly me and how I needed to look at my own behavior and one thing led to another."

Olivia smiled at her daughter. How far she'd come. "I'm so proud of you, Jenny. That was a really good thing you did."

Jenny smiled. "I just wanted to help Nick. I could see how upset he was. And that made me upset."

Olivia nodded. "That's how it is when you love someone. You feel what they feel."

"I do love him. And I figured things couldn't really get worse. She hadn't left her room since that breakfast at Iris's."

Olivia already had another tray of cookie dough balls ready to go. She got it into the oven to bake. "That was rough. I've been wondering how things were going since then but I was a little afraid to ask."

"I hope today is a turning point for them. I really do."

"It's a good day for it. Christmas Eve." Olivia wiped down the counter. "You know, we should get Yolanda something for Christmas. She won't have anything to open under the tree."

"I actually did, but then I'd decided not to give it to her because I thought she'd just think they were stupid."

"What is it?"

"A pair of leopard print slippers with these black sparkly flower accents on the front."

Olivia thought they sounded very Yolanda. "I bet she'd love them. I'd like to get her something, too." She looked at Jenny. "If I give you some money, will you go to the resort boutique and pick out something for me to give her? A pretty scarf, a bracelet, anything you think she'd like."

"Sure," Jenny said. "I'd be happy to do that." She got up.

"Take forty dollars out of my wallet. Doesn't mean you have to spend all of that, but just in case."

"Okay." Jenny went toward her mom's purse. "Then when I get back, maybe I can help you with the cookies."

Olivia's brows went up. "Yeah? You want to do that?"

"Do I want to make cookies with my mom on Christmas Eve day?" Jenny smiled. "I can't think of anything I'd rather do more."

Olivia smiled, mouth open and full of joy. "That would be great."

"I'll be back soon then. Don't bake them all without me."

"No chance of that." Olivia stood right where she was as Jenny slipped out, amazed by the idea that she might actually bake cookies with her daughter. When had that happened last? When Jenny was eight or nine, maybe?

To think that they were about to do that again seemed unfathomable. She felt a little weepy that such an activity could occur again. Only here. Only because of this place, and Iris's generosity, and all of the good that had come from her new life on this extraordinary little island.

She gave herself one more minute to feel emotional, then she put a big smile back on her face and got to work. The next batch of snowballs would be out soon. Those few minutes were her chance to get the peanut butter batter prepped.

Maybe Jenny could unwrap the Hershey's Kisses and then push them into the centers of the hot cookies when they came out of the oven. Olivia didn't care what she did, just that they were going to be together. It was all the gift she needed.

She sang along with the Christmas songs and by the time Jenny returned, Olivia had the snowballs done, the first trays of sugar cookies in the oven, and the tins lined with festive, red-striped tissue paper.

Jenny came in with a little bag from the shop. "Mission accomplished."

Olivia was washing out the mixing bowl so she could make more batter. "What did you get?"

"I went with the existing theme. I hope you don't mind." She walked into the kitchen and pulled the gift out of the bag. It was wrapped in tissue. She unwrapped it and held up a pair of dangly black and leopard Lucite earrings.

Olivia smiled. "Those are perfect. Thank you for doing that for me."

"It was kind of you to want to get her something."

"Have you heard from Nick?"

"Not yet." Jenny rewrapped the earrings and stuck them into the bag. "They must still be talking. If that's true, it's probably a good thing. Right?"

"I'd think so," Olivia said. "If the conversation wasn't going well, Yolanda would most likely be back in her room."

Jenny's eyes narrowed. "Or Nick is putting her on a boat back to the mainland."

Olivia made a face. "I really hope that's not what's happening."

Jenny pulled out her phone. "No messages. And I'm afraid to text him and interrupt." She put her phone away, smiling like she wasn't quite sure she felt it. "You know what? Let's just make some cookies. And when he's ready to tell me what's going on, he will."

Olivia tossed Jenny an apron. "Sounds like a plan."

Chapter Thirty-two

*A*ll of Iris's gifts were wrapped. Hadn't taken long. She'd bought the same thing for each of the girls, a beautiful present that she already knew they'd say was too much, but she didn't care. It wasn't too much. It was only a portion of what they deserved after everything they'd done for her.

For Vera, she'd arranged for her to take a cruise. Not just any cruise. An Alaskan one. Vera had talked about such a thing over the years. And now that Iris was doing so well, she could easily be by herself without Vera having to worry.

To make the trip extra special, Iris had paid for Vera to bring a companion as well. Anyone she chose. Iris knew Vera had some family scattered about. A brother in Illinois. Some cousins here and there. A niece and a nephew. Surely she'd be able to find someone to go with her.

With all of that taken care of, Iris decided to go out

for a walk. The exercise was good for her, she enjoyed it, and she liked seeing all the Christmas decorations that had been put up. It never hurt to interact with the guests a bit, too.

She put on her track suit and walking shoes and headed out. The sound of voices made her pause on the front porch. It sounded like Nick and Yolanda. She glanced up. Could they really be talking? The conversation was too muted for her to hear, but the tone sounded like an actual conversation and not an argument. That had to be good.

She shook her head, hoping for the best as she went down the steps.

She went by Arthur's Marina, smiling at the sign. How could she not? It was such a sweet thing to see. She continued on past the marina and headed for the bungalows. There were plenty of guests lounging on the beach.

It always amazed her that what felt like winter to her felt like summer to others. She knew it was all relative. If you'd come from Chicago in December, Compass Key's breezy, low-humidity seventy-something degrees would feel like paradise.

Which it was. No doubt about it. But to Iris, this was definitely winter. It was kind of fun to wear her little jacket and track pants. She felt sporty. Not how she usually felt in one of her caftans.

Maybe she should start wearing something else.

But she'd been wearing caftans for years. Decades, actually. They were so easy and cool in the heat. She supposed she might get a few that weren't so voluminous. Or maybe just some shorter sundresses.

Amanda had a good eye for things like that. Maybe she could help.

Iris waved to guests who waved at her, smiling and wishing them all a merry Christmas as she continued on her way.

She found Amanda at the front desk. There was no one in the lobby but there were a good handful of people shopping in the resort's boutiques.

"Busy day for the shops, hmm?"

Amanda nodded. "Hi, Iris. It sure has been. I even just saw Jenny a few minutes ago. And from what I can tell of the bags, David's cookbook is a hot item."

"It makes a great souvenir and a great gift."

She nodded. "He's going to have to sign another batch of them soon."

"Not a bad problem to have. You know, we should be selling Katie's books in there, too. Why aren't we?"

Amanda looked like she was about to say something, then just shook her head. "I have no idea. That's an excellent question. I'm going to look into that. Are you here to do some shopping, too?"

"No, I've got all of that done. I'm just out for a little walk, getting some air. Vera's making a cheesecake. A special one with some kind of sugar substitute that I can eat, she says."

"That's awfully nice of her."

"It is," Iris agreed. "I also wanted to ask you a question."

"Sure, anything."

"Do you think I could get away with wearing some shorter dresses? Sundresses, I mean. Now that I've lost some weight?"

Amanda smiled. "Iris, you can wear anything you like. It shouldn't matter what you weigh, just how you feel. You're beautiful in anything."

Iris laughed and patted Amanda's hand. "You're very kind. But it's important to me not to look foolish. I'm not a young woman. You understand what I mean. And I trust your style. Would you maybe help me pick some things out? We can look online. There are a few places I like to shop."

"I would be happy to."

"Thank you." Iris's hand went to the diamond at her throat. "Have you heard from your mother?"

Amanda's smile faltered for a moment, but she managed to hang on to it. "No, but it's okay. It's her decision. I'll be with Duke's family tomorrow afternoon, so I won't be alone."

"They're wonderful people, aren't they?" Iris was so pleased that Amanda had found Duke. He and his family were exactly what Amanda had needed.

Amanda nodded. "They have made such a difference in my life."

"I'm so glad. Well, I'm off to finish my walk. Merry Christmas and I hope I see you tomorrow."

"You will, for sure. Merry Christmas, Iris."

With joy in her heart, Iris continued on her way. She left the main building and followed the path toward the other side of the island where the main marina was. She didn't know if there'd be too much activity there today.

As she approached, she saw no sign of the resort's pontoon, glass-bottom boat, or Eddie or Rico. Obviously, the marina had plenty of activity.

She came to the fork in the path that would take her down past the outbuildings or cut in toward Phase II.

Since she hadn't been to Grant's studio in a while, she went straight ahead, deciding to stop in and see him. She didn't want to disturb him, though. If he looked busy, she wouldn't go in.

The garage door was up, so she peeked inside. He was standing in front of a canvas, but looking out toward the water, so he saw her right away.

He waved. "Iris! What a surprise. How are you?"

She smiled and went inside. "I'm wonderful. Just out for a walk and thought I'd say hello if you weren't too busy."

He met her a few feet in. "Your timing is perfect. I was just taking a break."

"What are you working on?"

He chuckled as he offered her an almost embarrassed smile. "A very rare thing. A commission. I take it you haven't heard?"

She shook her head. "I haven't."

He sighed. "Well, come have a look. I'll be done with it in a few days."

She walked around to see the canvas better. She squinted at all the pink. "Is that...Lala Queen?"

"It is. She's paying me a hefty sum, too. I can't lie, the money is nice. But Leigh Ann thought it would be a good idea not to upset Lala because of the bad press she might give us."

Iris squeezed his arm. "Oh, Grant. You're such a dear boy to think of the resort. I know this isn't your usual."

He smiled. "It's not, but there isn't much I wouldn't do for Leigh Ann or you."

"I appreciate it so much. I'm sure Leigh Ann does, too."

He nodded. "She's already said it several times."

"It's a lovely painting. Even if it is awfully pink."

He laughed out loud. "I'm going to keep my comments to myself. Probably better that way."

She grinned. "I won't keep you. I'm sure you're

eager to finish this one up. Have a wonderful Christmas, Grant."

"You, too, Iris." He kissed her cheek, and she kissed him back.

She wiggled her fingers in a little wave, then went out. It never ceased to amaze her what people were willing to do for the good name of this place. Grant was a terrific man. Another one of Arthur's investments that had paid dividends.

She walked back to the fork and took the second path this time, heading into Phase II. The landscaping was just beautiful. Anyone walking into this new area would think they'd arrived at the garden of Eden. She picked up the scents of plumeria and guava, maybe a hint of ginger in there, too.

This new section of landscaping had been especially designed to include fruit trees and plants. She knew there were groves of bananas, numerous guava, mango, and papaya trees, as well as lilikoi vines that had been planted. Herbs, like mint and rosemary, had been added in pots near the eateries.

She paused in front of Iris's, just to have a look at the sign again. It made her smile. It would *always* make her smile.

She imagined that somewhere Arthur could see it and was smiling, too.

Chapter Thirty-three

Since David was at the restaurant gearing up for the dinner shift, Grace met Curt at the marina's dock. Eddie was at the helm of the pontoon. He'd claimed he was going into town anyway. She hoped that was true. She hated to think he'd had to make a special trip, even if it was part of his job description.

"Hi, Curt. Thanks, Eddie."

Eddie gave her a nod as he tied the boat up. "No problem. There were packages to pick up anyway."

She saw the small pile of boxes behind him. "I'm glad that worked out."

"Me, too," Curt said. "I can't tell you how grateful I am for this."

Grace smiled. "You'll be a permanent resident here soon enough. This will give you a chance to get to know the place some."

"And David, too. Although I hate that I'll be interrupting your Christmas." He had a rolling bag and a big black duffel slung over his shoulder. He hoisted them onto the dock, then got off the boat. "Listen, I will happily get out of your hair tomorrow. I'll sit on the beach all day if you want me to. Eddie said I could borrow his tackle, so I might come over here and fish a little."

"Curt, it's Christmas. It's about being with people as much as it is about sharing time with family." All the same, she appreciated how thoughtful he was being.

Eddie got off the boat after him. "Nice to meet you, Curt. We'll have to see about doing some fishing sometime."

"I'd love that."

"You know where I am. Grace can point it out to you."

Grace nodded. "Sure. Eddie's just a couple doors down from us. I'll show you when we get close."

"Lead the way," Curt said.

She started walking, heading for the path that would take them through Phase II. It was nice to have that. It cut a few minutes off the old way of going all the way around. "I'm sorry about your place. Will you be able to save a lot of your stuff?"

"I hope so. I put everything I could up high, but it depends on how long things sit in that water." He shook his head. "What a mess."

"I bet. What happened?"

"All I know is that there was street construction going on right outside the apartment complex and they hit a main line. My building wasn't the only one affected."

"That sucks. Bad time of year for it."

"No kidding." He stopped walking to look at the two restaurants he'd soon be managing. "I can't believe I'm going to get to run these places. While living *here*."

She laughed softly. "I know exactly how you feel. Ten months ago, I was going through the same thought process."

"And how do you like it so far?"

They started walking again. Her smile stayed put. "It's been life-changing. And I don't mean that just in a superlative kind of way. It has literally changed my life and my relationship with David. Probably saved my marriage."

"Wow. I'm glad you guys worked things out. He's an amazing chef. So knowledgeable. And he seems like a great guy. I mean, he must be if you married him." Curt grinned.

"He's the best." She blinked a few times at how little that did to accurately describe what David meant to her. "He's better than that. He's my everything."

"It's none of my business, so please, feel free to tell me to shut up, but can I ask how this place saved your marriage? I've been divorced twice now, and I tried both times to make things work but..." He shrugged.

She felt for him. The thought of losing David had nearly devastated her. "Being here, and being around some of my oldest, dearest friends, was a real wake-up call for me. I was drinking way too much. I hate the word alcoholic, but it's a label that fits me. They pretty much had an intervention and set me on a better path."

"Wow. You?" He looked at her, clearly surprised and concerned.

"Yep. You know how it is in the restaurant business. End of shift drinks are part and parcel of the job, especially when you work nights."

"Yeah." He nodded. "They really are. How are you doing now?"

"I still have my struggles, but I've been sober ten months and being here really helps. All of my friends here know my issues. They help keep me on track."

"I'm really glad for you."

"Thanks."

He smiled. "Thank you for sharing. And now that I know, I won't ever tempt you with something you can't have."

"I appreciate that." She pointed. "That's us. That's Eddie down there."

"I can't believe I'm getting one of these to live in next month."

"Hey," Grace said. "Do you want to go see it?"

"Could I? That would be great."

"Sure. Let's put your bags in the house, then we'll walk over."

She unlocked the door then stepped out of the way to let him bring his things in. From there, they went over to the construction site.

She pointed to the two larger bungalows in the center. "These two have been designed differently. They each have four bedrooms and four bathrooms. They've been built specially to house more staff so that we can have more people onsite."

"That will be really helpful with Castaways being open so late."

"That was the thought process. We also want to build greater retention. Studies have shown that employees who are given housing tend to stay at their jobs nearly eighty percent longer."

He smiled. "I know I haven't even started to work yet, but I can see myself being here until I retire. Which might be never." He looked over his shoulder at the staff recreational area of picnic tables, grills, pool, and hot tub. "This is easily the best benefits package I've ever been offered."

"You haven't even seen where you'll be living yet."

"I'm not sure it matters. I'd take a tent at this point." He laughed. "But I would still like to see the bungalow."

"Come on." She went up the steps. Construction was done for the day, but she'd gone to get a key from

Amanda at the front desk before she'd gone to the marina. She'd figured Curt would want to see his soon-to-be new home.

She unlocked the door, then took a look toward both sides of the island from the porch. There was most definitely a water view. "It's not a direct view out to the water, but you can still see it."

He nodded. "It's the best water view I've ever had." Suddenly he laughed. "Sure beats the water view I have now."

She laughed, too, thinking it was good that he could joke about the burst pipe and the damage done to his stuff.

They went in. It looked livable but she knew there were plenty of odds and ends to be done and a final inspection to be had.

"This place is amazing." He walked in and did a slow turn, having a good look around. Of course, there was no furniture, which made the space seem bigger than it really was, but it was clear that the bungalow would be an easy place to live.

He pointed at the stairs. "Can I?"

"Sure."

He jogged up the steps while she stayed downstairs. "Two bedrooms, two bathrooms, pantry, laundry closet, everything you could want."

He leaned over the railing. "You know, I'd be happy to share this place if there was another employee who needed housing. It almost seems unfair that I should have this whole thing to myself."

"You're going to be working a lot of hours and shouldering a lot of responsibility. You're going to need a place to decompress and unwind."

"You're right about that. Still, I want to be accommodating. If sharing would help, I just want you to know I'm willing." He came back down.

"I'll let you know if anything comes up." It was a kind offer on his part. That kind of attitude would take him a long way here.

He rubbed a hand over his face, looking a little emotional. "Thank you." His voice caught. He cleared his throat. "You could have easily turned me down after what I did to you. I can't tell you what this means to me."

She smiled, feeling a little emotional herself. "If anyone knows the value of a second chance, it's me. Welcome to Compass Key. And merry Christmas."

Chapter Thirty-four

Leigh Ann had fixed an easy dinner of orzo pasta with shrimp, peas, and a light bacon cream sauce. It was simple, but indulgent. The perfect thing for Christmas Eve night. Now she and Grant were curled up on her couch, cups of decaf nearby.

Her little tree twinkled in front of the windows, adding to the atmosphere.

For dessert, she'd made chocolate mousse. It was from a mix, but she'd already tasted it, and it was really good. To make it fancier, she planned to add some whipped cream and sprinkled some crushed candy cane pieces over the top.

They had a movie on, *Holiday Inn*, and were both in sort of a blissed out, totally relaxed mood.

"Interested in dessert?" She asked.

"I might be." He looked at her. "Not sure I could do anything too heavy."

"Chocolate mousse with a little whipped cream and a sprinkling of crushed candy cane on top?"

"That sounds pretty perfect, actually." He straightened slightly. "Can I help?"

"Nope. It's practically made." She got up. "I'll just be a second."

He paused the movie.

She went into the kitchen and took out two of the four dishes of mousse that the recipe had made. She grabbed the can of whipped cream, then the candy cane bits she'd already smashed up.

She put a swirl of whipped cream on each dish, then sprinkled on some candy cane, and finally stuck a spoon in each one. She was no pastry chef, but it looked pretty festive to her.

The whipped cream went back into the fridge, then she carried the desserts to the living room.

There was a long, wrapped box sitting on the couch cushion she'd just vacated. "What's that?"

Grant looked at the box like it was a complete surprise. "I have no idea. I guess Santa was here."

She smiled but cut her eyes at him. "Grant Shoemaker. It's not even Christmas yet."

He shrugged, grinning. "I don't care. I can't wait any longer."

She put the dishes of mousse down on the coffee table. "What if I refuse to open it?" She wasn't going to.

Not even a little bit. But she wasn't going to give in so easily, either.

"Up to you. It's your present. I guess if you don't want to open it, I can't force you." He squinted his eyes. "Maybe I should just take it back if you don't want—"

She snatched the box off the couch and sat beside him. It was heavier than she'd expected. There was no way it wasn't jewelry.

From the size and shape of the box she knew it wasn't a ring and she was good with that. They'd had a serious heart to heart after Katie and Owen had gotten engaged and they'd both agreed that they were okay with not going down the marriage path just yet. Didn't mean they might not someday, but for now, they were happily committed to each other and completely monogamous and that felt like where they were supposed to stay.

At least for a little while longer.

"Go on," Grant said softly.

She pulled off the bow and the wrapping. Underneath was a black velvet box that looked like it might hold a pen or a bracelet. She opened it.

The breath slipped out of her lungs with a soft gasp that said it all. Inside was a gorgeous white gold diamond and opal bracelet. "It's beautiful. It's more than beautiful. I've never seen anything like it."

"You won't, either. It's an art deco piece, one of a kind, from 1935."

Rectangular links were each set with an oval opal that flashed with a multitude of colors. Each opal was surrounded by various shapes and sizes of diamonds, completely encrusting each link. The effect was somehow bold but feminine at the same time.

He lifted it from the box. "Try it on."

She held her wrist out.

He fastened it. "Opals have always reminded me of the sea. All those colors and the way the light plays in them. Like looking at the world underwater. And I thought, since there was no engagement ring to buy, that I should find another way to bring some sparkle into your life."

She just stared at it, turning her wrist to watch the stones catch the light. "I've never owned anything so beautiful. I mean that. It's clearly such a special piece, too. I love it. I love that it's old and has a history."

"You do?"

She nodded, almost tearful at his extravagant kindness. "I'm a little overwhelmed by how much. It's the nicest thing anyone's ever given to me. Thank you."

He smiled. "You're welcome. It was hard to find something pretty enough to go on your wrist."

She cupped his face in her hands and kissed him, the bracelet's glimmer catching her eyes right before she closed them.

He pulled her into his lap, holding on to her. "You

know what I realized when I was buying that bracelet?"

"What's that?" She held her arm up to look at it again.

"How much I enjoy spoiling you."

She laughed. "I think you've spoiled me plenty for a long time."

He shook his head. "There's a lifetime yet to go."

She smiled up at him. "You realize this means I can give you your present now." She was still very excited to give it to him, but she also knew it couldn't compare to the bracelet glittering on her wrist.

He wiggled his brows. "Bring it on."

With a laugh, she got up and went to the tree. The box was very heavy. She couldn't wait to see his face when he realized what it was.

She picked it up and carefully placed it in his lap.

He blinked. "Did you get me bricks?"

"Yep, that's right. Bricks." She giggled as she rolled her eyes. "Just open it."

He didn't hesitate, tearing into the wrapping eagerly. She'd used a sturdy Amazon box and stuffed it well with newspaper and tissue.

He opened the box, pulled the top layer of tissue off, and stared at the beautiful glass starfish. "But this... how did you..." He looked up at her, obviously surprised. "But this was sold when we went back to look at it again."

"It was." She nodded, quite pleased with herself. "To me."

A slow smile spread across his face. "I have clearly underestimated your deviousness. I'd like to say I've also never found you more attractive."

She laughed. "Good to know."

He shook his head as he took the starfish out. The colors were as spectacular now as they had been on that sunny day they'd first seen it. Blues and turquoise in all shades, bits of white and gold, all topped with flecks of iridescence and pearl set in clear glass. "I am blown away that you did this for me."

He stared at the object in his hands. "Do you know that I've thought about this starfish almost every day since we saw it? Mostly because I regretted not buying it when I had the chance. I knew she had others but the colors in this were just so perfect that it reminded me of the sea. I knew it would never be replicated. And a replica wasn't what I wanted anyway. I wanted *this* one. And now, here it is. Thank you."

She was all smiles. "I'm sorry you had to wait so long but I'm very glad it's made you happy."

"It absolutely has." He looked up at her. "But *you* make me happy."

She took her seat beside him again. "You make me happy, too." She picked up her chocolate mousse, the simple movement causing her bracelet to sparkle. "I can't get over this bracelet."

He eased the starfish back into the box, then put the box on the table. Before he sat back, he picked up his chocolate mousse. "This has been the best Christmas I've had in a long time."

She smiled as she spooned up some of the dark, rich mousse. "And it's not even officially Christmas yet."

He turned the movie back on and settled in next to her. "Well, we're officially out of gifts." He gave her a sly look. "I can think of other things to unwrap, though."

Chapter Thirty-five

Amanda woke up at her usual time, even though she didn't have to be up that early. Waking up at that time had just become habit.

But she wasn't going back to sleep. Not on Christmas morning.

Smiling, she stretched, then checked her phone. There was a message from Duke.

Merry Christmas. Come over when you get up and I'll make breakfast.

She grinned. They weren't exchanging presents until later tonight at his parents' house, but she was eager to see him. She was always eager to see him.

She texted him back. *Twenty minutes. And MERRY CHRISTMAS!*

She didn't wait for a reply, just got up and turned on the shower to warm up while she picked out something cute.

She went with cuffed jeans, a red-striped sweater,

and her white slip-on sneakers. After her shower, she dried her hair and put on a little makeup. It might be Christmas morning, when people traditionally hung around in their pajamas, but she wanted to look as good for Duke as she could.

Before she headed out, she texted him again. *Need me to bring anything?*

Just yourself, came his quick reply.

She smiled and put her keys and her phone into her pockets. She'd be FaceTiming with her kids later, but she could do that from Duke's house.

They knew all about him and had actually met him via FaceTime already. In private, they'd both told her how happy they were for her to have found someone.

It really was remarkable how much her life had changed. She locked her door and went over to Duke's.

He opened the door as she walked up his steps. He was wearing pajama pants, a long-sleeved Henley tee, and a Santa hat.

Her smile was instant. "Merry Christmas."

"Merry Christmas." He pulled her into his arms as she met him at the door, giving her a kiss. "This is how every Christmas morning should start."

"I agree." Some delicious smells reached her. Coffee and something else. "Are you making pancakes?"

"Yes. Blueberry. I know you don't usually indulge in things like that but—"

"It's Christmas morning and my boyfriend is cooking, so I'm indulging."

He grinned and pulled her inside, shutting the door. "Coffee's ready and there will be bacon, too. I figure since we aren't eating dinner until later, we needed a big breakfast."

She went into the kitchen behind him, headed straight for the coffeemaker. Duke already had two cups set out. She filled them both.

He went back to the stove where a large skillet held three pancakes. "What time are you talking to your kids?"

"They're supposed to call me. I told them anytime this morning was fine with me, so I'm not really sure."

"Maybe it's good we're eating early then."

She nodded. "Works for me."

"Want to go for a walk on the beach after we eat? If you get your call, we can come straight back here."

"I'd like that a lot."

A timer went off and he took a cookie sheet of bacon out of the oven. Her mouth was watering now.

"What can I do to help?"

He glanced over. "Hand me that cup of coffee."

With a laugh, she did just that.

He held his cup out and clinked it against hers. "Here's to a great Christmas."

She nodded. "It's starting off pretty good."

He winked at her. "It'll get better. I promise."

"Oh! I just realized I left your dad's book at my place. Michael put a lovely inscription in it."

"Thank you so much for doing that. We can get it later."

"Just don't forget."

"Trust me, I won't." He took the pancakes out and put them on a plate in the microwave that already held two. Then he poured more batter into circles and dropped blueberries into them.

She moved closer. "Just how many pancakes are you making?"

He shrugged. "As many as the batter gives me. Too many? Not enough?"

"Depends on how many you're going to eat, I guess. I think I'll be good with two."

"They're small."

She pursed her lips in an almost smile. "They're not that small. But okay, maybe three. Since we're not eating until later."

In a few more minutes, he had the last batch done and was filling their plates. She'd already gotten butter and syrup out. They sat at his small round table and dug in.

The pancakes were so good, and Amanda really felt like she was indulging. "These are great. I mean, surprisingly great."

"Hey," he said. "I'm a good cook."

"Yes, you are, but pancakes are a skill. And these are something special."

"Extra vanilla," he said. "Grace told me to do that."

Amanda nodded. "She would know."

After a few moments of silent eating, he sipped his coffee, then set it down and looked at her. "Any word from your mother?"

She shook her head. "No. It's not something that fills me with joy. Never will be. But I'm trying to accept that's just how things are going to be."

He nodded. "Sorry."

She smiled at him, even though it was a little weak. "It's okay. I mean that. Having my sister and my kids back in my life in a bigger way has helped a lot. So have you and your family. Your parents are great. So is Jamie. I'm blessed to know them all. And you. You know that, right?"

He nodded. "I do. My family loves you, too, you know."

"That's one of the great things about them. They are not shy about sharing their feelings or being demonstrative about them."

"I know that took some getting used to for you."

"It did. I wasn't used to it. But it's so much nicer than keeping things inside. Or having to wonder how someone feels about you." She thought about Denise. "The next time I see my sister, you know what the first thing is I'm going to do? Hug her."

He smiled. "When will that be?"

"I don't know for sure but we talked about it again. I really hope it's soon. I want to show her this place. And she's dying to meet you."

He laughed. "Am I going to have to pass some kind of test?"

"You've already passed it, trust me."

After they finished, she helped him clean up.

"You don't have to do that."

"Yes," she said. "I do. I want to."

He put the dishes in the dishwasher. "Just let me go change and we'll get that walk on the beach started."

"Perfect."

He went upstairs, coming back in the same shirt, but this time with jeans and flipflops.

She chuckled.

"What?"

"Men have it so easy. That's all."

He took her hand and kissed her knuckles. "I know I do."

She laughed. "At least you admit it."

They headed for the beach, hand in hand. It was a typically beautiful day on Compass Key, but somehow more so because it was Christmas. That one amazing day when anything seemed possible, the world felt swathed in kindness and love, and the simplest gesture spoke volumes.

The sand crunched beneath their feet. They passed

quite a few others walking hand in hand, too. It seemed a Christmas beach walk had been the thing to do.

Then a familiar couple appeared ahead of them, coming toward them. She squeezed Duke's hand a little harder. "Michael Gideon."

As the movie star and his wife approached, Amanda smiled at them, happy to see them hand in hand as well. "Merry Christmas."

"Merry Christmas," Kit said back.

Then Michael stopped. "Thank you again for getting us that massage this afternoon. We're really looking forward to it."

"I was happy that I could make it happen." She smiled up at Duke. "This is Duke Shaw, head of maintenance. His father, Jack, is the one I had you sign the book for. Duke is the one ferrying the massage therapists back to the mainland."

"Right," Michael said. "Thanks."

"Sure." Duke stuck out his hand. "Really appreciate you signing that book for my dad."

Michael shook Duke's hand. "No problem. Your dad's a big fan, huh?"

Duke laughed. "To give you some perspective, I was named after John Wayne and Dad thinks you're the next best thing."

Michael blinked. "That is high praise indeed. You think your old man would like a signed ballcap? I have a couple with me. They have the Gideon Productions logo on them. I'd be happy to get you one."

Duke nodded slowly. "He would be blown away by that."

"We're in Bungalow 17. Stop by after your walk and I'll get it for you."

"Thank you."

Michael nodded. "Sure. Great to meet you."

"You, too."

Michael and Kit went on their way. Amanda started walking again. Duke joined her, but he was shaking his head. "This place really is magic. And so is this day."

Amanda just smiled. "It really is."

Chapter Thirty-six

Christmas was fun for adults, but no one enjoyed it like a four-year-old, Katie thought.

Dakota was currently knee-deep in wrapping paper, hugging the doll she'd just gotten. Gunner was in his bouncer, chewing on a soft, squishy ring meant for just that.

Josh, Christy, and Sophie all sat in the living room watching the carnage. Gage was running a few security checks. Rika was in the kitchen fixing Christmas breakfast, which she'd said was going to be waffles and a ham and cheese casserole.

Katie was sitting at the breakfast bar with Owen, having coffee.

Hisstopher perched on the entertainment console under the television, keeping an eye on things. It was clear he was curious, but not so curious he wanted to be floor-level. He'd already gotten some catnip toys, a package of treats, and a new cat condo.

Which was almost exactly what Fabio had gotten.

Katie's phone went off. Just the low buzz of an incoming text. She picked it up and had a look.

A group message from Iris. *Merry Christmas to my wonderful girls. I love you all. If you're able, please come see me today to exchange presents.*

Katie looked at Owen. "Iris saying merry Christmas and that she'd like to see all of us girls today to exchange gifts."

He nodded. "Maybe you could go after breakfast."

Christy looked up. "If you need to go somewhere, I can guarantee you that after we eat, this one," she nodded at Dakota, "will be well occupied playing with all these toys for quite a while."

"Okay. I'll go after breakfast then." Katie sent Iris a text back. *Merry Christmas! I love you all. See you after breakfast, Iris?*

That's fine, Iris replied.

"Speaking of breakfast, it's almost ready," Rika said.

Gage came in from the back of the house, making eye contact with Owen. "All good."

"Thanks," Owen said. "And you're just in time to help me set the table."

As the men got to work doing that, Katie went into the kitchen to see what she could do to help.

In a matter of minutes, they were all sitting down at the table and eating Rika's delicious meal. The ham and cheese breakfast casserole had sun-dried tomatoes and was baked on top of a layer of hashbrowns. The waffles were fat and fluffy and, in true Rika-style, she'd served them with three kinds of toppings. Strawberries, salted caramel, and hot fudge. She'd offered ice cream, too, if anyone wanted.

Dakota had been the only taker.

They lingered over breakfast, in part because it was so good, but also, at least for Katie, because the moment was so very sweet. She wanted to save it in her memory bank for the rest of her life. Her first Christmas breakfast with her son and her grandchildren. And her fiancé.

Finally, Christy pushed her chair back. "I'm going to see if I can get Gunner down for a nap."

Josh nodded. "I'll keep an eye on Dakota."

"Dakota and I are going to color," Sophie announced. "Then maybe later have a swim."

"Wait for me," Katie said. "I'll swim with you when I get back from Iris's."

"It's a deal," Sophie said.

Katie gave Owen a kiss. "See you when I get back."

He nodded. "Taking the boardwalk?"

"Yes. After that breakfast, a little bike ride will be good for me."

He smiled. "Give Iris my love."

"I will." Katie headed out through the back of the house and took the little path that led to the boardwalk that connected the two properties. She hopped on her bike and rode to the other side. The sun was bright and the day clear, although cool. She didn't mind the coolness at all. If there was ever a day for it, it was today.

She parked at the end and left the bike at the start of the boardwalk, then went to the house. Leigh Ann was already headed up the steps, a shopping bag filled with presents in her hand.

"Merry Christmas," Katie called out.

Leigh Ann turned. "Merry Christmas." She waited for Katie to catch up. "How are you?"

"Really good." Katie pointed to the stairs. "I need to run up and get my gifts, then I'll be down."

"Okay, see you inside."

Katie went up to her place, grabbed her gifts, and went back to the first floor. Amanda, Olivia, and Grace were already inside, sitting in the living room with Iris. Vera was with her, too.

Vera got up as Katie entered. "Coffee, anyone? Or would you rather a little low-carb eggnog? I made it myself."

Katie laughed. "You really did go all out. I'll try a small glass."

Vera went into the kitchen as Katie took a seat next to Leigh Ann.

Iris smiled at them all. "First of all, Merry Christmas to all of you."

"Merry Christmas," they all said back.

"I asked you all to come by because I wanted to give you your presents."

Olivia instantly shook her head. "Iris, you've given us enough to last us a lifetime. Literally."

"Agreed," Katie said. "Although I'm ready to do the gift exchange." She'd gotten a signed book for everyone, each book tailored to their individual tastes, along with a beautiful, handmade, beaded bookmark.

Amanda raised her hand. "I second that. You have definitely given us enough."

Iris laughed. "Well, be that as it may, you're getting gifts anyway. This is the first time in many years that I've looked forward to Christmas. I wanted to get you something for giving me that feeling again. Something you would always remember me by. I promise I will never be this extravagant again."

"Extravagant?" Leigh Ann said. "I'm not sure I like the sound of that."

Vera handed Katie a small glass of eggnog. "You know how she is. Once she gets an idea, there's no stopping her. Much like the five of you."

That got some laughs.

Iris got up and retrieved five small boxes from under the Christmas tree, where Calico Jack was currently curled up. She handed a box to each of the women. "This is my way of saying thank you for everything you've done and everything you're going to keep on doing to preserve the home that Arthur and I built. I know he would approve of your work and this gift."

Katie looked around at the other women, exchanging a curious look. Then she opened the gift along with the rest of them.

An almost collective gasp went up as the boxes were opened.

Katie stared at the smaller version of Iris's Escape Diamond. But it was smaller in a very limited sense. The stone in front of her was plenty large. She shook her head. "This is just a replica, right?"

"Cubic zirconia," Olivia offered.

"No," Iris said. "It's a real three-carat diamond. A mini-Escape, if you will."

"It's too much," Amanda said.

"It's so beautiful, but it is definitely too much," Grace agreed with a kind of breathless appreciation.

Katie took the necklace out of the box and held it up so that the stone dangled free on the white gold chain. "Iris, I...don't have words. This really is too much, but I know there's not a chance in heaven that you'll take it back. So thank you."

Iris was beaming. "Put them on. If you want, of course. I don't mean to tell you what to do. I just wanted you to have something to always remember me by."

Grace laughed. "In case an island and a resort

weren't enough? Oh, Iris. I don't even know what to say."

"You don't have to say anything." Iris lifted her coffee and took a sip.

Katie was overwhelmed. She managed to fasten the clasp around her neck before the first tear slipped out. The fact that Iris had done this for them was so very Iris. The incredible gift that Iris had given them, not just the necklace, but *everything*, hit Katie all at once.

The fact that she was spending Christmas with her son, the biggest blessing that Katie had never expected to receive in her life, was all down to Iris.

Katie got up, walked over to Iris, and hugged her. "Thank you. For everything. I love you."

Iris patted her on the back. "I love you, too."

Chapter Thirty-seven

Olivia walked back into her bungalow where Eddie was waiting on her. He was in the kitchen, washing up the breakfast dishes, which made him the best boyfriend ever. Actually, he'd earned that title a while back.

She set her shopping bag on the floor by the tree. All of the girls had come up with such wonderful gifts. They'd all seemed to like her rain jackets, too.

She went into the kitchen.

"Well?" He turned and gave her a look. "Everything okay?" Then his eyes widened, and he pointed at her throat. "You weren't wearing that before."

"Nope." She shook her head. "I sure wasn't. Iris gave us all replicas of the diamond Arthur left for her."

Eddie nodded, smiling like that made sense. "Ah, a replica. So that's just glass."

"Oh, no," Olivia said. "It's real."

His eyes went wide again. After another second or

two of staring, he said, "There's no way you approved that."

She laughed. "I don't control her personal money. Just the resort's money."

"Oh. Right. Of course." He blinked. "But man. Wow."

"You can say that again." She touched the diamond, needing to be sure it was still there. It hadn't really sunk in that such a rock was hanging around her neck. She was adding it to her insurance tomorrow. "I can't imagine what this cost. Actually, I can. I hope she knew someone that was able to get her a good deal."

He wiped his hands on a dish towel. "I don't think Iris has ever cared about good deals when it comes to things like that."

"You're probably right." She let out a long breath. Not in a million years would she have guessed Iris was giving them something like this. "I don't know what to do. I've never gotten such an extravagant gift in my life."

"There's nothing for you to do but to accept it graciously." He came out of the kitchen to join her. "I know Iris well enough to know that she never gives any gift with the idea that it will get her something back in return."

Olivia nodded. "I know, you're totally right. She definitely didn't give us these with any kind of strings attached. Although we did get to give her our gifts."

He took her hand, lacing his fingers through hers. "And you named the new restaurant after her. So you've already, as a group, done something that touched her very deeply. I'd say you're on pretty equal footing."

"But naming that restaurant for her cost nothing."

He shrugged. "Isn't that what Christmas is all about? Or should be? It's not about who bought the biggest gift or spent the most. It's about giving something that tells the recipient you thought long and hard about them. That you thought about them. Didn't Iris give you her explanation as to why she bought you all those diamonds?"

She nodded. "She did and you're right. You couldn't *be* more right. I'm just overwhelmed by the gift, but I need to focus on the thought behind it. Thank you for reminding me of that."

"You're welcome. How about we exchange our gifts, then take a little Christmas boat ride, just the two of us?"

She nodded. "I'd like that." She really would. It had been a long time since she and Eddie had been out on the boat together by themselves.

"Come on," he said. "Let's go see what's under the tree."

"I'm going first." She picked up the biggest box and handed it to him. It was the coffeemaker she'd gotten him.

He took the box and sat on the couch, grinning with all the enthusiasm of a little boy. It was adorable.

She sat beside him, watching.

He unwrapped the present and his smile got bigger. "This is fantastic. Look how fancy! I need a new coffeemaker."

"You *really* need a new coffeemaker." She pointed at the box. "And it has an espresso maker, which you can apparently also use to make Cuban coffee."

He studied the box a moment before letting out a little gasp of happiness. "So it does. I can't wait to try it out." He looked up. "You really do love me."

She laughed. "Yes, I do. Now it's your turn to pick a gift."

He got up and came back with a little box wrapped in sparkly blue paper with white snowflakes, which was the only snow she'd see this year other than what was on television. "Here you go."

She unwrapped the gift and found a pair of blue and green enamel sea turtle earrings. She put them on, since she wasn't wearing earrings. "I love them! They remind me of this place. And they go perfectly with my work shirt."

He nodded. "That's what I was thinking."

She gave him the Cuban coffee next, and in return, he handed her a box that contained a ballcap that said "Captain" on the front of it and had her name embroidered on the back. She smiled. "I'm going to wear this every time I drive the boat."

"Today, then," he said.

"Yep." She put it on. She loved it. And Eddie was the reason she could drive a boat now, so it was even sweeter coming from him.

It was time for his big gift. The watch. She got the box out from under the tree and put it on his lap. "There you go."

He weighed it in his hands. "Feels expensive."

She snorted. "It could be beach rocks for all you know."

He shrugged, his eyes full of amusement. "I like beach rocks."

"Then you're about to be very disappointed."

"I doubt it." He unwrapped the watch. "Is this... Oh, wow." His mouth curved up in a smile. Then he started laughing.

That was not the reaction she'd expected. Not even a little bit. "What's so funny?"

He sighed and shook his head, still chuckling, as he put the watch down and went to get something from under the tree.

He came back with a package and handed it to her. "Open it and you'll understand."

She slipped a fingernail under the tape and pulled the wrapping off a very familiar package. She blinked, looked at the box underneath, and started chuckling. "You got me the exact same watch."

"The lady's version," he said. "Someday you might be out on the water by yourself. I want you to be safe no matter what. I thought this would help."

She looked at him, still smiling. "That's why I got *you* the watch. Plus it has all those bells and whistles related to boating. Stuff I have no idea how to use, to be honest."

"I'll teach you." He leaned over and kissed her. "I guess this is proof we're meant to be together, eh, *mamacita*?"

She nodded. "I guess it is."

"What do you say we get our watches set up and go test them out?"

"Sounds like exactly how I want to spend the day."

"What time are we supposed to be at Nick and Jenny's?"

"Not until six."

"Plenty of time for a little cruise then." He kissed her again. "Merry Christmas, my love."

"Merry Christmas, sweetheart."

Chapter Thirty-eight

Grace walked into the bungalow, arms full of gifts, to find David on the couch watching football, something he enjoyed but didn't often get time to do. "Hi, honey."

"Hi. How was Iris's?"

"It was...well, you're not going to believe this." She put the gifts on the kitchen counter and went over to him.

He sat up a little. "Believe what?"

She joined him on the couch. "Notice anything different?"

"You might be a little prettier than when you left. How do you do that?"

She laughed and poked his arm. "Thank you but I'm being serious."

He started to shake his head, then his gaze dropped lower. "New necklace?"

She knew instantly he didn't know it was real. "Yes. What do you think of it?"

"It's very sparkly."

"Do you know why it's very sparkly?"

His eyes narrowed. "Because that's what rhinestones do?"

"Okay, true, but this is not a rhinestone."

"Cubic zirconium or whatever then."

"Not that either."

He shrugged. "I give up."

"It's a diamond."

He stared at her throat. "You mean a *real* diamond?"

She nodded.

"But it's so big."

She laughed. "Not compared to the one Iris wears, which this is supposed to be a copy of. A smaller copy, obviously. Can you believe it? She got one for each of the girls. Something for us to always remember her by."

"Because the island and the resort aren't enough?"

Grace nodded, still snickering. "That's what I said!" She sat back on the couch. Diamond earrings *and* a diamond necklace for Christmas. She felt so fancy. "That woman is too much. I've never known anyone so generous."

"I'd have to agree with you on that." He settled in next to her.

"How's the game?"

"Good," he said. "It's been nice just to hang out and watch it and not have to think about what time I need to get ready."

She looked toward the back of the bungalow. "Where's Curt?"

"He went out for a bit. Said he wanted to walk around and get to know the place a little. Mostly I think he wanted to give us some alone time. Which was nice of him, but I don't want the guy to feel like he has to disappear. It's his Christmas, too."

"I told him that yesterday. I'm sure he'll be back when he's ready." She patted David's knee. "How about I get that charcuterie board together? Might be nice to have something to nibble on, huh?"

"That would be great. Any food I'm not in charge of sounds good, actually." He grinned.

"So I could just make you a bowl of popcorn?"

"If I don't have to make it? Heck, yes."

"I'll keep that in mind." She snorted and went into the kitchen. She pulled out a big wooden platter, then got out all of the ingredients she'd bought to go into the display. She rolled some of the meat slices, folded others, and turned even more into fancy "roses" to decorate the platter.

She cubed some of the cheese, while some got sliced. The small log of goat cheese went on whole with a cheese knife beside it. Into small dishes arranged on the platter, she put a variety of olives, some pickled vegetables, and some salted nuts. She added a little dried fruit, too. Apricots, dates, and fat golden raisins.

When she finished the platter, there was enough food to feed an army, but they'd be grazing on it all day.

She took out a second, smaller platter and fanned out crackers, pita chips, and Melba toast.

She carried the charcuterie board over first. She was pretty impressed with the end result. She set it down on the coffee table. "Ta-da!"

David sat up, giving it his full attention. "Now that's what I'm talking about. Nice job, honey. That looks amazing."

He pulled out his phone. "I'm posting this. Mostly because it will make people jealous."

She laughed as she went back to get the crackers and some little plates and napkins, bringing all of that back to the table as well. Then she returned to her seat next to David.

As she did, the door opened, and Curt came in. "Hey. I'll just be a minute."

"Curt, you don't have to leave again," Grace said. "You're more than welcome to hang out with us and watch the game."

He shook his head. "I don't want to intrude."

David waved his hand like that was silly. "Come

watch the game. Look at all this food Grace just put out. We can't eat it by ourselves. Besides, I was thinking we could talk a little shop during halftime. I have a couple ideas I'd love to run past you."

Curt hesitated. "That is a pretty amazing spread. You sure you wouldn't mind?"

"Please," Grace said. "Come join us and help us eat all of this."

Curt smiled. "Okay. Thanks."

David pointed to the empty recliner. "Take my chair. I'd rather sit here with Gracie anyway."

Curt gestured toward the guest room. "I'll go change and be right back."

As Curt went through the bedroom door, Grace hugged David's arm. "Thank you for making him feel welcome."

David smiled. "I'm just buttering him up so he won't pass out when I tell him all the work I have in store for him."

She laughed. "I see how it is. Well, I should tell you now that we're not talking shop at halftime."

"We're not?"

"No. We're opening presents."

He glanced toward the guest room. "Won't that be a little weird for Curt?"

"Don't worry, I got him a couple things from both of us."

"You did?" David smiled. "Nicely done."

"Nothing much. A Mother's T-shirt, a Mother's travel mug, and a box of those Key Lime chocolate creams. All of it from the boutique."

"I love those Key Lime creams."

She smiled. "Don't worry, there's a box of them under the tree for you, too."

He kissed her cheek, pulling her in closer. "As wives go, you're pretty amazing."

"I know," she said, giving him a wink. "I guess that means you have to keep me."

He nodded. "Oh, I plan to. For a long, long time."

Chapter Thirty-nine

Jenny couldn't get over the change in Yolanda. Since the long talk she and Nick had, Yolanda seemed like a different woman. Calmer. More smiley. But most of all, more at peace. Not just with herself but with everything.

Jenny didn't think Yolanda had complained about a single thing since that conversation. How that was possible, Jenny didn't know, but then again, she'd had a pretty big attitude adjustment herself here on Compass Key.

She knew firsthand the power of this place. And the power a frank discussion could have. She was giving Christmas a little credit, too. This was the time of year for reconciliations and mending fences.

And, hopefully, for successful attempts at Christmas dinner. She'd never done one before. Never done any kind of big meal like this, but here she was, about to cook her first turkey with all the trimmings. Stuffing, mashed potatoes, gravy, carrots, and rolls.

For dessert, she'd picked up a Key Lime pie. Eddie, who would be coming with her mom, had volunteered to bring a dessert, too, so they were covered.

Nick had already said he'd take care of peeling and mashing the potatoes, although Jenny was pretty sure that wasn't something he'd done before, either.

In fact, she'd caught him watching an instructional video on the subject on YouTube, which had been so adorable she'd about melted.

What a guy.

Besides her mom and Eddie, Iris, Vera, Leigh Ann, and Grant were all coming, too. It seemed only fair to invite Iris and Vera, since they lived in the same building. Vera was bringing green bean casserole. The good kind, Vera had said. Not the traditional goop. Her words. Jenny didn't care what kind Vera made, she knew it would be good.

Leigh Ann and Grant were bringing cranberry sauce and deviled eggs, which Leigh Ann said was a tradition she'd grown up with.

Jenny had asked all of the women. Katie and her sister already had plans to be at Owen's with Katie's family. Amanda and Duke were headed to his parents'. Grace had said she and David weren't leaving the house, except for maybe a walk on the beach.

Jenny understood. Those two worked a lot and probably wanted a total day of doing nothing.

Jenny had taken the turkey out of the fridge earlier. Now the oven was hot, and she needed to prep the bird. She unwrapped it, patted it dry, then rubbed it all over with butter and a nice dusting of salt and poultry seasonings. She'd found those instructions online and they'd had a lot of stars, so fingers crossed.

She hoisted the bird onto the rack in the roasting pan, then carried it to the oven where she centered it, then closed the door.

She turned the light on and took a long look at it, not expecting anything, just saying a little prayer over it that it would at least be edible.

She took a couple of photos and posted them to her own social media. After that she went to shower and wash her hair, getting herself ready except for her outfit, which she wasn't going to change into until the last minute, just to be sure she didn't spill anything on herself.

Even with an apron on, she didn't want to take any chances.

Back out in the big living room-dining room-kitchen area, taking care of the table was next. Even though it was still early, she wanted to get it set and looking pretty so she wouldn't have to worry about it later when everyone started to arrive.

She was using the simple dishes that had already

been in the house, but she'd bought a Christmas table-cloth and a pair of red tapers to go in the brass candle-sticks she'd found. With white napkins and some green beaded napkin holders she'd found at the thrift shop, the table would look nice. Simple, but that was okay. The food would be the star.

She hoped. At least she knew dessert would be good.

With the table dressed and looking beautiful, she decided to peel the carrots. It was probably too early, but she needed to keep her hands busy, or she'd be opening that oven again and she knew she wasn't supposed to do that until it was time to baste.

The rolls would be easy enough. They were crescent rolls from a can. Today was not the day for her first attempt at breadmaking. She doubted anything she could make could compare to those buttery crescent rolls anyway.

Nick walked in, sweaty from the run he'd just taken. "Hey. You look busy."

She nodded. "I probably should have gone to the gym like your mom, but I feel like I have so much to do and if I don't stay in this kitchen, none of it's going to turn out right."

He walked over. "I know you're nervous about this dinner, but it's going to be great. You ace everything you do."

"I appreciate the vote of confidence, but I've never

done anything like this before." She put her hands on her hips and took a breath. "My mom always made it look so easy. Of course, she was only cooking for three of us, but still."

"You could always call her, you know."

Jenny shook her head. "No. I want to do this on my own. I want to show her that I'm capable."

"Don't you think she already knows that?"

She smiled at him. "Yes, but I want to prove it to her. I want her to be proud of me."

"Babe, I know for a fact she's proud of you." He glanced at the oven. "Whether or not the turkey skin is burned isn't going to change that."

Her mouth fell open. "How can the skin be burned? It's only been in there an hour." She ran to the oven and looked in. The bird looked no different than when she'd put it in.

Behind her, he snickered.

She poked him in the arm. "Nicholas. Don't do that to me."

He laughed and held his hands up. "Sorry. I couldn't help myself. Off to shower."

"That's a good place for you, you smelly beast." She glared at him while trying not to laugh.

A few minutes after he headed for the bathroom, his mom came in. She gave Jenny a quick smile. "I'd be happy to help you with anything you need after I take a shower."

"Thanks, Yolanda. So far I feel like I'm in good shape, but I'll let you know."

"All right."

"How was your workout?"

"It was good." Yolanda's smile warmed up a bit. "I feel like I can indulge now."

"Good," Jenny said, once again hoping there'd be something to indulge in.

As Yolanda went in, Nick came out with damp hair and rosy cheeks from having just been in hot water. "Did I hear my mom?"

"Yep. She just came back from the gym and went to shower."

"Okay. Do you mind if I put the game on? I don't watch much football but it seems like the thing to do."

Jenny laughed. "Go ahead. Maybe it'll be a good distraction."

He turned the TV on and found the right station, but instead of sitting down he came into the kitchen. "Could I start peeling those potatoes? I figure I can do that while I watch."

"Oh, sure. Okay. Hang on." She got the big pot out and the bag of potatoes and set them on the counter for Nick.

He was rummaging in a drawer for the peeler. "Babe?"

"Yes?"

He straightened. "What's a peeler look like?"

She suppressed a smile. Even she knew that. She went over to the drawer and had a look. But after digging through all of the utensils, there wasn't one. "Must be in another drawer."

Ten minutes later she'd searched every drawer in the kitchen. "It never occurred to me to buy one."

"No problem," he said. "I'll run down to Iris's. I'm sure Vera has one."

"Vera probably has several. Thanks."

Jenny exhaled as he headed down the steps. She pressed her hands to her stomach. A small crisis easily averted. Hopefully nothing major would crop up.

He was back in a few minutes, peeler clutched in his hand. "All right, I'm ready to work."

"Great."

He walked back to his spot at the counter. "Any tips?"

"On peeling?" She chuckled. "You know you need to wash the potatoes first, right?"

"Sure." He said it with such exaggeration that she knew he was fibbing. But something about his unwarranted sense of confidence helped ease her nerves.

Whatever happened with dinner, it would be fine. What mattered was being together. And being with family.

And this Christmas, Jenny had that more than she'd ever had before.

Chapter Forty

*L*eigh Ann had trained Rita this morning, promising her the one workout even though it was Christmas. After that was done, she'd come straight home and made a quick breakfast of scrambled eggs and bacon. Then she'd called both of her children and wished them Merry Christmas.

She'd sent them and their spouses all Mother's T-shirts, but also generous gift cards so they could buy whatever they wanted. Investing in Owen's OM coin had been a very wise move. Between that, her divorce settlement, and moving here, she had more than enough money to spoil them.

She checked the time. She was doing fine. Grant was supposed to be here by three, although they weren't due for dinner at Nick and Jenny's until six.

How sweet of Jenny to invite them.

The only possible fly in that ointment was Yolanda, although Leigh Ann had heard from Olivia that the first Mrs. Cotton had had a change of heart. Leigh Ann hoped for Nick's sake that was true and not just another scheme of Yolanda's.

Honestly, it would make all of their lives easier if they could stop worrying about that woman and whatever her next threat might be.

Leigh Ann didn't want to think about Yolanda anymore, though. Right now, she wanted to focus on making her deviled eggs to take to Christmas dinner. They'd been a tradition in her family growing up. In the South, you had deviled eggs for every occasion, from a christening to a funeral. So naturally, that included holidays, too.

She'd boiled her eggs a couple days ago so they'd be ready to go today. She got the bowl out of the fridge and went to work peeling. She'd put football on the television, another tradition in her house growing up. Her father had always watched the games on Christmas Day.

It was a sweet memory.

One by one, she took the shells off, thinking about past Christmases, her life now, and how blessed she was. It was easy to lose herself in the simple activity and happy recollections.

With the eggs peeled, she was about to start slicing them in half and getting the yolks out when someone knocked on her door. She wiped her hands on a towel and went to answer it. Grant was there, all smiles.

"Merry Christmas, beautiful."

She threw her arms around his neck and kissed him. "Merry Christmas. How's your day been so far?"

"Better now." He laughed. "It's actually been really good. I've been at the studio for a couple hours this morning and I've just about finished Lala's painting."

"Really?" She let go of him so he could come in. "That was fast. Although I know you've been working pretty hard on it."

"I still have another day or two to go, but as it happens, Lala wandered into the studio this morning while I was working and took a look."

Leigh Ann almost held her breath. "And?"

His smile was radiant. "She loved it. She loved it so much she brought her manager and her assistant in to see it. And..." He reached into his jacket pocket and pulled out a long slip of paper.

Leigh Ann took a closer look. It wasn't just a slip of paper. It was a check. For a quarter of a million dollars.

"She's giving me the second half when the painting is done." He tucked the check away. "Thank you for getting me to do this. That money will go a long way."

"Toward refinishing your boat?"

"That but also a few other things. I'm going to finally get an ecommerce store built onto my website so I can do online sales."

"I love that. I'm surprised you don't do that already."

"I should be, but getting a store set up properly and securely isn't cheap. It could mean hiring more help at the gallery, but that shouldn't be a big deal." He hesitated. "I have another idea, too."

"Oh? What is it?"

"I was thinking about doing...a calendar. What do you think? Would people want to look at my work all year round?"

She clapped her hands together. "Yes! I think that's brilliant. We will absolutely sell them in the boutique."

"It wouldn't be for this coming year, obviously, but the one after. I need time to research it, find the right printer, figure out which of my works should be for what month and all of that. But this money will help me afford that project."

"That's great."

"You're great." He kissed her. "I mean it. Thank you."

"You're welcome." She smiled at him. "I'll be happy to push you into doing more things you don't want to in the future."

He laughed. "For now, would you mind if I just sat and hung out a bit? I know we have dinner at six, but is there anything else you need me to do?"

"Nope. I'm making deviled eggs to take over. Make yourself at home. You can put whatever you like on the television, too."

"I'm happy to watch the game."

Her eyes narrowed. "You like football?" She hadn't really seen him watch that many games of any sport. Maybe a few in passing, but he never seemed to care too much one way or the other.

"I like some. Football, especially. Some tennis. Hey," he said. "I'm an all-American man, you know."

"I do know. Have a seat and relax. Once I get these eggs done, I'll join you."

"I look forward to it."

She went back to the kitchen and back to her eggs. She got them sliced in half, popping the yolks out into a separate bowl, where she mashed them then stirred in some mayonnaise, salt and pepper, a helping of sweet relish, and a little bit of yellow mustard.

Once that was done, she carefully spooned the mix back into the hardboiled whites, then added a sprinkle of paprika for color.

She put the container of deviled eggs into the fridge, then cleaned up and joined Grant. She sat beside him on the couch.

He turned the volume down a little. "Were you able to talk to your kids this morning?"

"I was. It was really nice."

"Any chance you'll get to see them in person soon?"

"I don't know. Probably easier if I go to them."

"So why don't you? At some point you should be able to take a few days off, right?"

She nodded. "I've thought about it. Both the spa

and the fitness center are doing great. I need to hire another personal trainer, but I'd planned to do that after the new year. I suppose once I make that happen and get that person trained, I could take some time off."

She smiled at him. "You want to go with me?"

"Do you want me to?"

"Yes. I'd love for you to meet my kids."

He grinned. "I'd be happy to go. Let's do it. You pick the dates and let me know, I'll make it work."

"Yeah?"

"Yeah."

She kissed him. "Thanks. I love you."

"I love you, too." He put his arm around her.

She settled in next to him, more content than she'd ever been in her life.

Chapter Forty-one

*A*manda was on a high from talking to her kids, but that didn't stop her from sensing the curious vibe in Duke's parents' house. She felt it as soon as she and Duke walked in, but she chalked it up to Christmas. It wasn't a bad feeling, but just like there was something more going on than would be on a typical day.

She supposed that was exactly the right kind of feeling for Christmas and decided to ignore it and make herself useful instead. She had a shopping bag full of presents, just like Duke did.

As soon as they were through the front door, a skinny tan and white dog came racing toward them, almost running into Duke. He gave the dog a scratch on the head. "Hiya, Goose. Merry Christmas."

Amanda gave Goose a little scratch, too. "Who's a good boy? Goose is."

Duke held out his hand toward her bag of presents. "Do you want me to take those?"

Amanda smiled. "Why? So you can shake the packages with your name on them?"

He laughed. "Maybe."

"I'll take them to the tree myself." She looked at Goose. "There might be something in there for you, too." There was. She'd gotten Goose a new toy, a stuffed Santa.

They walked through the kitchen where Dixie and Jamie were working on the meal they were about to have, and the smells made Amanda's mouth water.

Dixie greeted them with a big smile. "Merry Christmas!"

Duke gave them each a hug. "Merry Christmas, Mom, Jamie."

Amanda followed, wishing them the same. Jack came in, giving his son a look, then focusing on Amanda. "How are you?"

"I'm great, Jack," she answered. "How are you?"

"I'm always good."

She smiled. He was. She'd never really heard him complain about a thing. He was going to get such a kick out of his presents later.

"Are we ready?" Duke asked his dad.

Jack nodded. "We are."

Amanda didn't know what they were talking about.

Dinner? They couldn't be eating this early, could they? It had to be something else.

Duke took her hand. "We have a surprise for you."

She looked up at him. "We? As in all of you?"

He nodded. "Yep. It's in the living room."

"Okay." A weird mix of nerves and excitement swirled through her. Duke looked so serious.

As if suddenly realizing that, he smiled, squeezing her hand. "It's all good, I promise."

He led her into the living room. Jack, Dixie, and Jamie followed. The tree looked beautiful with all of its hand-made ornaments. She put her bag of presents down. There was nothing in the room that looked like a surprise.

Jack cleared his throat. "Come on out."

Amanda didn't understand who he was talking to until she saw movement out of the corner of her eye.

She turned to see a woman standing in the doorway that led to the bedrooms. She stared for a moment. "M-mom?"

Her mother gave a little nod, hands clasped in front of her. "Hello, Amanda."

"If you two would like to sit outside and talk," Jack said. "We'll give you all the time you need."

Amanda nodded as Duke and his family went back to the kitchen, but she couldn't take her eyes off her mother. "What are you doing here?"

"If you don't want me here—"

"It's not that," Amanda said. "I just don't under-stand. We haven't spoken in months. You never respond to any of my texts. I've given up trying to call. And now you're here?"

Margaret nodded. "Dixie reached out to me on Thanksgiving." She took a few steps into the room. "I didn't want to talk to her, either, but that would have been impolite."

Whereas not talking to her daughter was appar-ently fine. Amanda tried to keep an open mind.

Margaret went on. "She said how nice it would be to see me again, which I believed to be a lie, but I also find Dixie to be a rather genuine person. Perhaps too much, at times. Then Jack reached out to me. As did Duke. Even Jamie sent me a text."

Amanda glanced back toward the kitchen but none of the Shaws were visible. "And that led you to come here?"

"There was a lot more conversation. Some with your sister, as well. I understand you two talk on a regular basis."

"We do. Our relationship is really good."

"That's nice," Margaret said softly. "The Shaws are a very persuasive bunch." She took a breath but just stood there like she was searching for her next words. Or maybe she knew what they were but couldn't make them come out.

Amanda said nothing, letting her get to wherever it was she needed to be.

Finally, Margaret exhaled. "I regret how things ended between us. I realize that you're an adult and free to make your own choices. Choices I need to learn to respect."

It was Amanda's turn to be speechless. She found her voice. "Maybe we should go sit outside and talk."

Margaret nodded. "I'd like that."

"Me, too."

Together, they went out into the backyard and sat at the table.

Amanda shook her head. "I can't believe you're really here. Are you staying here?"

"I am," Margaret said. "The Shaws have graciously given me their guest room."

"I just don't understand how they pulled this off. You weren't talking to me. I didn't think I'd ever talk to you again. What changed?"

Margaret stared at the table. "I guess I did. Talking to Dixie and Jack helped, too. I know I was hard on you growing up. I thought it was the only way I could be if I wanted my children to end up with any chance at a successful life."

Margaret sniffed. "You and Denise have definitely done that. Had successful lives. And I can see now that it was despite me, not because of. I failed you. I am sorry for that."

"Wow." Amanda breathed the word out so softly she almost didn't hear it herself.

"The more I spoke with Dixie and Jack, the more I realized I was the one suffering. Not you. You went right on living your life. And living it well, as I've heard from them. Meanwhile, I was so wrapped up in being right that my life came to a grinding halt."

She exhaled a ragged breath. "I'm an old woman, Amanda. An old, foolish woman. I have no relationship with you and Denise only tolerates me. Maybe it's too late for me to change. But I am sorry."

Amanda reached out and took her mother's hand. "Do you want to change?"

Margaret looked into her daughter's eyes. "I do. I'm not sure how. But I know I don't want things to go on as they have been."

"I don't either. I guess we'll just have to figure it out together, huh?"

They sat and talked and cried until Duke opened the slider and stepped outside. "I don't want to interrupt. I just wanted to see if either of you needed anything."

Amanda wiped her eyes and looked at her mom. "I think we're good." And for the first time in her life, she really meant that.

Her mom patted her hand. "We are." She smiled at Duke. "Thank you. Is it dinnertime? I don't want to be the reason the food gets cold."

"Just about," he said.

Amanda stood. "We should come in and help. Maybe freshen up a bit."

Her mom got up. "That's a good idea."

Duke just nodded. "Whenever you're ready."

Amanda and her mother went in. Amanda splashed a little water on her face, being as careful of her makeup as she could, then dried her face, cleaned up the smudges of mascara her tears had caused, and ran some fresh gloss over her lips.

She'd never be able to repay Duke and his family for the gift they'd given her. They'd done the impossible, at least for her it had been.

It was enough to make her tear up again. She blew out a breath and regained her composure.

Jamie called everyone to dinner, so Amanda went right to the table in the dining room. She sat next to her mother, happily, still very much in disbelief that she'd come to Florida. And that the Shaws had not only orchestrated the whole thing but also kept it secret.

That gave them a lot to talk about during dinner, which was delicious. Afterwards, they went back to the living room to open gifts before dessert.

Duke stood. "Before we get started, I have a confession to make."

Amanda couldn't imagine what it was.

"I had an ulterior motive in getting your mom down here."

"Oh?" Amanda still didn't know what he was talking about.

He nodded as he reached into his pocket and pulled something out. Then he was down on one knee in front of her. "I wanted her blessing before I asked you a very important question."

Her mouth came open. There was a diamond ring in his fingers.

Duke smiled. "Amanda, you're the missing piece I've been looking for. I love you and I can't imagine my life without you. Will you marry me?"

For a moment, there was no air in her lungs, then her voice came back to her. "Yes. I will."

Chapter Forty-two

If Christmas day was filled with excitement and surprises, then Christmas evening was filled with the kind of warm happiness and contentment that only family, good friends, and unconditional love could bring.

Iris was blessed to have all of those. But as she sat at the big round table at Nick and Jenny's, she could only pray they did, too. Yolanda had been quiet and rather meek since everyone had arrived, but Iris really couldn't tell if that was an act or the real thing.

She prayed it was a true change of heart and that Nick and his mother could now move forward in a much healthier way.

Dinner was running a little late, but no one seemed to care.

To her left was Leigh Ann with Grant next to her. Nick was beside him, then Yolanda, then Jenny, then Olivia, then Eddie, then finally, to Iris's immediate right, Vera. Or rather, they would be. Right now, Olivia and Jenny were in the kitchen about to bring dishes to the table. Nick was taking drink orders.

Leigh Ann and Olivia were both wearing their new necklaces, which pleased Iris immensely. Olivia was also wearing a fancy new watch, while Leigh Ann's wrist sported a very sparkly bracelet.

"I take it you girls had good Christmases?"

Leigh Ann turned toward Iris while leaning into Grant. "The best."

"You can say that again," Olivia answered from the kitchen. "It's been a fantastic day. How was yours, Iris?"

"Mine was wonderful. I had so many marvelous presents from you girls. I felt absolutely spoiled, I tell you." She looked across at Yolanda. "And you, Yolanda? How has your Christmas been?"

She nodded. "It's been nice. I'm just happy to be here." She smiled over at Nick. "With my son. And all of his new friends." She took a breath. "I'm grateful that you allowed me to visit, Iris. I really am. I want you to know that. You gave me a gift without even realizing it."

She sounded sincere, Iris thought. That was good enough for her. "I'm glad to hear the trip has been a good one for you."

Nick brought more drinks to the table. Right behind him was Jenny with a magnificent-looking turkey, browned and crispy. She set it in the middle of the table. "There's plenty more coming."

Olivia brought the stuffing, and in a few more trips, she, Jenny, and Nick had everything else on the table and were taking their seats.

Iris stood. "Would anyone mind if I said a blessing?"

"No," Nick said. "I think it would be nice."

Iris smiled and bowed her head. "Thank you, Lord, for the blessing of this family and these friends and for this bounty before us. I pray you'd give us all a healthy and happy New Year. Amen."

Amens echoed all around the table. Eddie crossed himself.

Nick stood up, carving knife and fork in hand. "I've never carved a turkey before, but Jenny's never cooked one, either. If she can do that, I can do this."

With great encouragement from everyone, he went to work. Before long, dishes were being passed and plates were being filled.

It didn't take long for the compliments to start coming. The food was delicious and Iris was impressed. "This is really your first turkey, Jenny?"

She nodded. "It is."

"Well, it's done to perfection. You should be proud."

Vera's fork stopped midair. "I couldn't have done better myself."

Olivia was all smiles, too, Iris noticed. And why wouldn't she be? Jenny had done a fantastic job. It was certainly something for a mother to be proud of.

Iris felt the same way about all five of her girls. About the job they'd done for her. About the way they'd left their comfort zones behind and started new lives here on Compass Key. What courage and faith that had taken.

What heart and drive and determination.

They were so brave. And now, it seemed they were very much reaping the rewards of the risks they'd taken.

As the meal wound down and waistlines felt a little tighter, a loud buzzing sounded.

Vera nudged her. "Your phone."

"Oh," Iris said. "I guess it is."

"Mine, too," Olivia said.

Leigh Ann held hers up. "Group text."

Iris took out her phone and opened the message to see a woman's hand with an engagement ring on it and the words, *I said yes!!* underneath.

She gasped and looked at Leigh Ann. "Is that what I think it is?"

Leigh Ann nodded, all smiles. "Amanda and Duke are engaged."

Olivia let out a happy sigh. "That's just great. Good for them."

Another buzzing preceded a second picture. This

time it was of Amanda and her mother. The message read, *I'll explain more later but the engagement came with her blessing. The Shaws are my Christmas miracle.*

Olivia was shaking her head. "Can that really be true that Amanda's mother is there? She's even smiling."

Iris nodded. "It must be true. If anyone could pull off that reconciliation, it's Jack and Dixie." She looked across the table. "But then, there was a pretty major change of heart here this week, too, wasn't there?"

Yolanda smiled. "Yes, there was."

Olivia showed Jenny the photos Amanda had sent.

Jenny's brows went up. "That's quite a ring."

Nick got up and went to lean over her shoulder to see the pics. "Oh, I don't know. I mean, it's nice, but do you think it's as nice as this one?"

He pulled a ring from his pocket and showed it to her.

Jenny stared at it for a second, then burst into tears. "Are you...asking me..."

He bent one knee. "Yes, Jenny, I am. I am so crazy about you it hurts. Please spend the rest of your life with me."

She nodded, still crying, managing to get out a soft yes.

Olivia was weeping now, too. Iris glanced at Leigh Ann, who was wiping her eyes. So were Yolanda and Vera. In fact, Iris's own cheeks felt wet.

She sniffed. "Isn't this grand? I wish you all the best." She smiled. "I do love a good wedding."

"Me, too," Vera sobbed.

"And now we have three of them to look forward to." Iris glanced heavenward, her mind on Arthur and the magic he'd created here on Compass Key. He'd given her all kinds of new things to look forward to, new reasons to get up every morning, a new family, because that's what all of these people were to her now.

It was almost like he'd known what he was doing for her when he'd created this place. And maybe he had. He'd always been an incredibly thoughtful man.

Olivia suddenly lifted her glass, her gaze on Iris. A soft smile curved her mouth as a knowing look came into her eyes. "Here's to Arthur Cotton, without whom none of this would be possible."

All around the table, glasses were raised.

With a warm heart and a grateful spirit, Iris lifted her glass. "To Arthur. And to Christmas. God bless us everyone."

Want to know when Maggie's next book comes out? Then don't forget to sign up for her newsletter at her website!

Also, if you enjoyed the book, please recommend it to a friend. Even better yet, leave a review and let others know.

Other Books by Maggie Miller

The Blackbird Beach series:

Gulf Coast Cottage

Gulf Coast Secrets

Gulf Coast Reunion

Gulf Coast Sunsets

Gulf Coast Moonlight

Gulf Coast Promises

Gulf Coast Wedding

Gulf Coast Christmas

About Maggie:

Maggie Miller thinks time off is time best spent at the beach, probably because the beach is her happy place. The sound of the waves is her favorite background music, and the sand between her toes is the best massage she can think of.

When she's not at the beach, she's writing or reading or cooking for her family. All of that stuff called life. She hopes her readers enjoy her books and welcomes them to drop her a line and let her know what they think!

Maggie Online:

www.maggiemillerauthor.com
www.facebook.com/MaggieMillerAuthor

Made in United States
North Haven, CT
26 August 2024

56573411R10183